CLIMBING OVER GRIT

CLIMBING OVER GRIT

by
Marzeeh Laleh Chini & Abnoos Mosleh-Shirazi

l'Aleph

Marzeeh Laleh Chini & Abnoos Mosleh-Shirazi

CLIMBING OVER GRIT

Published by l'Aleph – Sweden – www.l-aleph.com

l'Aleph is a Wisehouse Imprint.

ISBN 978-91-7637-553-2

© Wisehouse 2018 – Sweden

www.wisehouse-publishing.com

© Without limiting the rights under copyright reserved above, no part of this publication may be reproduced, stored in or introduced into a retrieval system, or transmitted, in any form or by any means (electronic, mechanical, photographing, recording or otherwise), without the prior written permission of the publisher.

*To the strongest women I know,
my mother Najma-Mahnaz and my sister Jaleh.*

Chapter 1

It is said that the greatest memories are the ones you will never forget, but it is fairly the opposite for me.

I think the flashes of bad memories are stronger and more painful. They burn deeply inside your thoughts. They walk with you all day and yell at you all night. You can't even sleep. But when you do, they haunt you in your dreams, turning them into nightmares. These bad memories are the most loyal companions. They always emerge from the corner of their presence.

My father was a small, short man who had hair only around the sides of his bald head, with little eyes and a big round nose on his small, round face. He shaved every day, but left a moustache. He always wore handmade suits with clean white ironed shirts, and polished his shoes every day. He also wore thick, round glasses and could not see very well without them. My father was always reading or writing something, and had to bring the books or papers very close to his face to be able to read them even with his glasses on.

My father was born in 1921 in the city of Shiraz, Iran. He was a very educated man. Men of his generation were fortunate to be educated as far as the sixth grade or even go to school at all. But my father was a smart young man. He was hardworking and passionate about reading, regardless of the subject, which eventually got him his degree in literature and theology. The opportunity to receive education of this level was limited to ministers, senators, and royal families, among other big names. Despite his endeavors, he didn't encourage his own children toward education.

If you ask anyone what would make one a good father, most of them would say one who gives love, attention, and time and is tolerant. I understood the difference between education and knowledge ever since I was a child. Money or education never turns a man into a good father. Yes, my father was an educated man, but knowledge was something he did not have. He did not know anything about love, he did not know anything about caring, and I am certain, he did not know a thing about tolerance.

And yet, I could not be too harsh on him. He was from a wealthy yet peculiar family. His father married several times, and often had multiple wives at the same time. My father had so many siblings that I wonder how he remembered all their names. I just called all of them Aunt and Uncle and used secret titles to distinguish them. One of them biked everywhere, and my siblings and I knew him as Uncle Bicycle. The other one turned red every time he laughed, and we called him Uncle Beet secretly. The interesting part is that my father was the only educated person in his entire family. They always looked down on my father. They were already so rich that they considered education to be a waste of time.

I always respected my father. I always tried to find the good in him. I loved him. But in real love, there would have been more hugging, playing, laughing, and perhaps more attention and more presence. He mostly came home when we were sleeping, and left the house early before we were awake, so we would not see him in the mornings or at night. I guess I always waited for him to miss me, and to maybe want to spend a day with me, but that never happened. Still, I loved him.

My mother was a tall, beautiful woman with large hands and feet. She was always in shape, dressed nicely, and had neat hair. She was born in 1932 in Shiraz, and was eleven years younger than my father. She never liked reading, but she had a very good memory and knew many poems by heart. My siblings and I loved it when she recited poems for us because it was the only time we could spend with her. It felt very good to sit beside her quietly and just listen. She liked knitting too, and was good at it. She never liked to have maids, because she believed they would gossip about her personal life. Keeping face was all that mattered to her. She never bothered to keep our home clean or feed us properly. To her, spending time and money on food and fruits was a waste. This belief, however, only applied to her children. She always ate well. To her, giving birth was the only importance of motherhood. She preferred eating before us, or ate after we were finished. Alone, quietly, and privately in the kitchen, she ate better food than she gave us. But at night, if Father was home for dinner, she cooked, and we all ate together. She never got involved deep in any problems. If there was anything that could bother her even a little, she would just walk out of it easily. She always had a saying that problems are like toothache, just pull out the bad tooth and the pain is gone. But *What would people say?* was a much bigger question to my mother than, *What is wrong?* The saying, "Never judge a book by its cover" reminds me of my mother. Everyone envied her. Everyone wanted to be her. She pretended to have a wonderful marriage, and no one could ever reach her level of happiness. They never saw how much her life lacked love and passion. Having a popular husband, attending royal parties, having dinner with important people of the country, and owning unique jewelry made her fake happiness look real. She was always excited to meet ministers and senators. She even visited the king and the queen and was very proud about that. It was a great subject to talk about with others for years.

She would never cook anything proper for us, something like traditional Persian meals with mouthwatering stews, rice, kababs, or freshly baked cookies, or any vegetables aside from salad. When we were hungry, we were to cook an egg, or she would heat up some beans and we would eat them or grab a piece of bread if we were very hungry. Our wealth did not improve the quality of our food. Our fruits were always close to being completely rotten. Yet, my mother always had fresh food and fruits to eat, but when it came to us, it didn't matter. She supposedly had a "weak" stomach and couldn't take the poor-quality foods that were available for the rest of us. She would make my father go to the market and buy her fresh meat and ripe oranges or any fresh seasonal fruit, and we would watch her eat while we ate our usual boring beans. We even felt sorry that she was sick, and we were happy that she was eating healthy food. My mother cooked fancy foods when we had guests, but her cooking wasn't as good as what we tasted in the homes of our other family members. At least we got the chance to eat meat when we had guests. My father didn't pay much attention to it. He ate whatever was available.

Sometimes I think I should not blame her either. She lost her father when she was only six. Her brother was ten, and her two sisters were only two years, and six months. Her mother was an extremely religious woman who never remarried. My grandmother inherited multiple lands from her wealthy husband and her father, but she never wanted to spend money, and she had her reasons for that. She wanted to take care of everything until her minors were grown-ups and hand them their wealth. But, she never realized that she was breaking down the morale of her children. So my mother grew up poor in a wealthy family. For that reason and because she was forced to marry my father, my mother never forgave my grandmother, even on her deathbed.

My grandmother married off my mother when she was fourteen. And because she was so religious, she picked a man from a very religious family as well. My mother never met my father until the wedding night. This was not too unusual in those days. It was on her wedding night when she realized that my father was very short, and she was very tall, and he wasn't very handsome, and they would never look good together. I am not saying that my father was an ideal man, but I guess my mom never gave him a chance. Things never worked out, and she hated him until the end. After this, my mother had complete control over my grandmother. I remember my grandmother being afraid of my mother; she'd try hard to take care of everything for her to keep her quiet and satisfied.

She hated her mother and her husband. But she loved one person: her brother. He was a dream man: handsome, tall, kind, social, and very well respected. He threw grand parties for every possible occasion. In mother's eyes, he never wasted time on books and instead spent valuable time with his family. He appeared at every family reunion, which my father never had the time for. My mother's brother lived next door with my grandmother. Our other neighbors were my mother's two sisters. They all bought houses next to one another with their inherited money. And each of the three sister's husbands lived in the house that his wife owned. We always spent a lot of time in their houses to play with our cousins and spend time with our grandmother.

My uncle was very different from the rest of my family. Everything was just different in their house. He knew how to spend his money smartly, and comfortably and well at the same time. His house always smelled like a bakery or a fancy restaurant. My uncle's wife would take the time to prepare the most remarkable feasts that seemed like they were stolen from a king's dinner table. The house was spotless. It was always tremendously clean. The garden had beautiful flowers and vegetables with not a single weed in it. You could see how much she involved her kids in her life and made them do everything with her. She was as beautiful as a Hollywood actress. She was always in great shape, with a very kind smile. It was not easy to live with my grandmother and be a neighbor to three sisters-in-law. But she was raised in a very high-class family with great manners and never complained. She made me realize how much of a difference there was between my mother and the rest of our family. I was always astonished by how elegant and magical everything my uncle's wife did was. I wanted to grow up and become as great of a housewife as she was. She was simply extraordinary.

It was not just the food she cooked that was spectacular, but it was also her home decor. All their furniture seemed like it came directly out of movies and fancy catalogues. My mother and father had as much money as they did, but my uncle and his wife lived very lavishly. They always strived to live life to the best of their abilities. They looked as rich as they were, and I always wished I was their child.

Although my uncle's life seemed perfect, it lacked love. There was no chemistry between him and his wife. They respected each other unlike my parents, but it was still empty. Love is something I was taught by my second aunt Roohi. My aunt Roohi was a tiny and very kind woman who always had the same short haircut. My aunt Roohi and her husband really loved each other, and their love filled their home, so much that you'd feel it along with happiness, generosity, respect, and kindness the moment you walked in. I always thought to myself how great it would have been if the two peoples' lives I idolized the most would combine into one. That is what I wanted my life to be like. My aunt Roohi's husband was a broad-shouldered man with a big wide face. He was a gentleman because of his generosity toward his wife and kids. It was unheard of for a man to wash dishes or cook and clean at home after his own hard day of work back then. Men were expected to be tough, the kind with bad morals, horrible personalities, and rough attitudes. It was considered shameful and embarrassing if a man helped his wife at home. When Aunt Roohi developed a skin problem, even though she had maids, her husband helped her with all the love in the world in any way that he could. He was very proud to help his wife. He was a funny guy, capable of making jokes out of any situation. When we were around him, time passed by quickly. It was strange to see a man like him because everyone I knew was so serious. The way he carried himself made everyone actually respect him for helping his wife around the house so much, and being there for her in ways she did not even ask for. He was the kindest man I ever knew. I do not call him a wonderful husband because he washed dishes, but because he cared for and loved his family. He was unforgettable. That is why I always thought to myself, even as a child, *Why don't all men get inspired by his respectful actions and reenact them?* I wanted to take good characteristics of people and apply them to myself. I wanted a life that was a combination of my uncle and aunt Roohi's family. Yes, in my dreams, life could easily be this simple and beautiful.

My second aunt Mah was the most beautiful among her sisters. Her life was completely different from everyone in the family. Her husband was a rich and successful merchant. He was a young bald man with a heart disease. I never saw him smile. I was disappointed when I looked at him and by the way he treated my aunt Mah. You would never imagine a woman so innocent and kind be forced to silence by such a harsh man who was blinded by his power. He never hit her, but he ignored her. He wouldn't talk to her for months, and if he did talk to her he'd humiliate her in front of others. He always looked at her like she was stupid and dumb, and it was a waste of time to listen to a woman. The way he disrespected her was worse than beating her. She was silenced by fear and acted according to his demand. I remember wishing that some of Aunt Roohi's husband's love and attitude would somehow travel into his closed mind and blossom into happiness and kindness. Her silence, patience, and innocence could bring a tear to anyone's eyes. She inspired me to never give up. Her beautiful smile in every harsh circumstance taught me how to conquer the challenges in my life with a sword of laughter. Her husband was so religious that no one could walk into their house without a hijab, completely covered from head to toe, which was also called a chador. Not even my grandmother had such rigid beliefs compared to his. Life was so serious and tough at their house that it made us reluctant to go there, even though we were all neighbors. Anytime we wanted to see her, we would make sure her husband was not home. She was not allowed to go anywhere without her husband's permission, which was never granted. He always had a group of people invited in their home for business matters, and my aunt was too busy washing and cleaning and cooking. She always looked so skinny and pale, but you could feel an angel hidden inside her somewhere.

My aunts were nothing like my mother. You could easily see that they possessed real character as great mothers for their kids, were kind daughters for their mother, and were wonderful sisters for one another.

My mother on the other hand, was sculpted by an ego and always demanded love and attention, and had no love to give in return. I grew up to learn that God's gift to me was a good memory. I should say that this was unfortunate. I remember every detail of my life since I was three. It might have been a privilege if those memories were worth remembering. Or maybe it was just meant to be, so I could share them one day with the world. Still, sometimes I wish I had the power to forget bad memories. I think at some point in life, this is what everyone wishes for.

When I was three, I had two sisters and a brother. Amene was the eldest of us all. She was born in 1948 and was four years older than me. She had white porcelain skin and a round face like my father, but a small nose and beautiful eyes like mother. My brother Zein was born in 1950, the second eldest sibling. He looked more like my mother in a short figure. I was born in 1952 and was named Najma, which means *star*. My face has features from both my mother's and father's faces. My sister Masume was born two years after me in 1954. She was petite and pretty. None of us three sisters looked alike at all. We had three different countenances.

One thing my mother did care about was how we dressed. She had great taste. We wore couture clothes and beautiful shoes. She always tied my sisters' and my hair in nice girly pigtails with cute ribbons that matched our dresses. We always looked neat. We were very polite, and maybe the politeness was a result of how quiet we were. I don't know how the four of us had become so quiet and harmless by that point. If it were up to my parents' influence, then we'd be shaped into attention-seeking, unbearable children. But influence didn't play a big role in our lives. My mother was always sad and depressed. She never showed it when she was around people; she was social and funny, always capturing everyone's attention. But, at home, it was a different story. We were never allowed to get too close to her. We didn't disturb her, or ask any questions, or make any loud noises by running or playing too much like the other kids. My father was barely around, and my mother was emotionally never there. So, we started to learn how to be actors, to never share our feelings or talk about our problems. We kept everything inside and were never ourselves. All I learned from them was that parents give you life, clothes, and food, and you should be grateful for just that and expect nothing more. My siblings and I were mostly taken care of by our grandmother and we loved her. She was short, and had obvious lines of life's path on her dewy face. Her hair was mostly white and some gray, and always covered by her hijab. She was only twenty-five when my grandfather died of an epidemic disease. Since then, she had had a very difficult life, but never really complained about it. She was a very patient woman. I think this was partly because she was so religious. She devoted everything to God, but took it a little bit too far. She made sure that we did all the tasks of a good Muslim, but through this she made a monster out of God. Every step that we took we had the fear that we might go to hell for it. I see God from a completely different perspective than they did. I think Islam is far greater than just wearing hijabs, praying three or five times a day, and fasting. I think those are important practices, but we shouldn't forget that it's also about having a good character, being kind, loving, generous, knowledgeable, wholesome, and the best you can be to yourself and to the people surrounding you. In my Islam, there is acceptance and understanding. There's love and there's freedom. There's no harm or wage wars. I think God meant for it to be as simple as that.

Maybe my grandmother thought she was doing what was best for my mother when she married her off to my father. But of course, the main reason for the marriage was religion. The unfortunate part of it all was that he was religious in a completely different way. It's kind of like an egg. Some like it sunny side up, some like it scrambled. But it's still an egg. As a result, my father and my grandmother never got along and never really liked each other, but there was mutual respect.

One thing my grandmother and father agreed on was the importance of performing hajj in Mecca, something all capable Muslims must do at least once in their lifetime. In 1955, my father decided to make the difficult trip to Mecca. He wanted to go while he was still young because back then, traveling to Mecca was not as easy as it is today. Instead of a short comfortable trip with airplanes, nice hotels, and air-conditioned buses and taxies, most of the trip was spent walking and on camels, donkeys or crowded buses, depending on how much money you had. The pilgrimage took three months because at the same time they traveled to Iraq and Syria, to visit the graves of former Imams who were well respected by Shia.

The thought of him leaving made my siblings and me anxious. What turned the anxiety into fear was that we knew that a trip to Mecca back then was called a "trip of death." Many pilgrims never came back, losing their lives to many kinds of maladies. And once they left for Mecca, there would be no news of them for three months. I didn't know if I'd get a father back or a corpse.

Grandmother really pushed my mother to make the trip with my father. Because performing hajj was mandatory, my grandmother believed my mother might as well do it with her husband, where she could be safer since it is a long and dangerous journey, and no woman should go alone for their safety. Surprisingly, my mother did not want to leave us behind for three months. In the midst of all this, I don't think my grandmother was thinking about us four little kids as she was trying to convince my mother to take a trip with possibly no return. I wondered what would happen to us, if Mother and Father didn't come back. My siblings and I needed them. We loved them even though they never really talked to us, or played with us, hugged us, or loved us. There was an innate longing for my mother and father to just be there, alive and present. However, in my grandmother's eyes, religious duties were more important than this. Maybe she thought this trip would change my mother. Or maybe she didn't realize at the time that kids have feelings too and break a little. Our hearts were smaller and our patience, little. The only way we could have protested was to cry. After much convincing, my mother decided she'd go to Mecca with my father, leaving Amene, Masume, Zein, and me alone with our grandmother.

And so they left.

Days kept passing by, and I missed them. I didn't know if they were okay or in trouble. We couldn't know. There was no way to communicate with them. During every sunset, I'd go up the stairs that led to our flat roof, and I'd sit beside the little window, and look out at the street and the orange sun. I sat wondering about my mother and father. The days felt long, as if the earth had stopped spinning. I couldn't focus on myself and I couldn't play; I was too anxious. Amene and Zein played like usual, and seemed like nothing had changed. I was the only one who cared that our parents were gone. I guess it should have been the same for me too, since Mother and Father were not really involved in our everyday lives to begin with. Despite this, I'd constantly ask my grandmother where my mother was, and every day she'd remind me that my parents were coming home soon. She soon grew tired of hearing my question, and one day she replied, "You know what? She's not coming home because of you. You did something bad and your mother is not pleased with you. It's because of you she hasn't come back." Every word stabbed me; I was only three. I ran up to the window before the rooftop again and prayed. The sky was dark, but the stars shined the light of hope. I looked at the biggest star and wished for it to send a message to my mother, telling her that I didn't know what I did to disappoint her, but I did know that I was sorry. I promised her through the star that if she came home I would never do a single thing to make her leave again. I believed somewhere in my heart, that my mother could hear my voice and that she would forgive me and come home.

Weeks passed, and it was all the same waiting, crying, wondering, apologizing, hoping, and praying. And at last they came home.

But Mother had lost so much weight that I could not recognize her. It was my father, and then a woman, a stranger. The blistering sun of Saudi Arabia had dimmed her skin. Her expression was fragile. This was unlike her. I don't know if my father missed us. He hugged us for a second, and left. Zein and Amene ran to my mother and hugged her. They crowded her for hours. I couldn't. I stood at a distance, and watched. I refused to go near her. I was afraid of her. I wanted my real mother to come home. No one really noticed how I felt, not even my mother. She didn't notice that I was distant.

Eventually things went back to normal, but I never got closure from the experience.

Chapter 2

As Amene, Masume, and I were engaged in a game of dress-up, my mother interrupted us with a thrilled expression on her face. "Tell Zein to come here. I have a very important announcement to make," she said.

When Zein joined us, she told us that she had a gift for the four of us. We would no longer be a family of just six. My mother was pregnant.

As my mother left to continue along with her work, thoughts began running through my head. I wondered if it would be a girl or a boy, and how I couldn't wait to play house, and pretend to be the baby's mom. Just thinking about a new baby made me smile. Mother looked much happier, and that was most important to me. A new baby meant a new life for us. And I couldn't wait.

That same year, I turned four. There are so many milestones you hit before your twenty-somethings. Until then, you can't wait to grow up. Then you hit an age when you've molded. Instead of growing taller each year, you just grow older. Age is nothing but a number now, but as a child, age was pride and power. I wish I wasn't so eager to grow up. I wish I was four for longer.

It was 1956, when my mother gave birth to a cute baby boy, my little brother Ebrahim. His every move was captured in our hearts. He brought a kind of happiness into our home that I had never experienced before. But this happiness only surrounded me. My father was expressionless. I couldn't tell if he was excited about his new son or not. It was hard to see my father's happiness, but very easy to detect his anger. My mother was happy, but only for a short period of time. Soon after giving birth, her depression came back. A lot went on during the time that Ebrahim was born, so much that the joy of his birth was slowly suffocated by the complications around it.

Money came easily in my family. Both of my parents inherited their wealth, and were stable in finances with lands that were left for them. Money always became a competition between my mother and father. Whenever we fell short, they would argue about who should spend their money and sell properties. This always crossed the line into violence and abuse. My father wasn't much of an investor. He never focused on growing his properties and having something to leave for his kids. Instead, every time money was needed, he sold a property just to keep my mother quiet. Either way, neither of them understood that properties don't grow like vegetables. If you keep selling one every time you're stuck, you will soon lose them all and end up with nothing. They were so focused on proving to be the richest in the relationship, that they slowly wasted each other's wealth. They didn't realize they were cutting the branches we all were sitting on. My father was very miserly. That's probably why all their fights over money led to hitting and screaming. He hated spending. Since the day of their marriage, they were living in a house that my mother owned, even though he could afford a bigger and better one. Every single day my mother reminded him that he was living in her house. It seemed like revenge when my mother pushed my father to sell properties. The problem was that he'd sell his land cheap just to get it out of the way, and stop her nagging, and get her off his back for a while. Even if my father was careless enough to lose everything, my mother could have been smart enough to keep them and do something better with the money.

Just like my father's family, my mother believed his education was a waste of time and money. She was always against anything he liked to do or ever did. She never supported him in his passions, even though his education was what brought us more money and popularity. Every conversation turned into a fight involving chasing, screaming, throwing objects at each other, and really no useful conclusion. Nonetheless, my father always did what he wanted. One of the greatest things that he did was to build a private kindergarten in Shiraz. This was an achievement far beyond our understanding because not only was there no private schools in Shiraz at the time, but there were no kindergartens either. There were only a few public schools, and all of them started at first grade. My father's school became a quick success, which made him extremely rich and famous. It boosted his ego to a level higher than it already was. Not only was it the only kindergarten in the city, but it was also very luxurious. It provided students with many extracurricular activities, and even had "music time" every day. I remember that there was a young, blind man in a neat suit, who played the violin. I found him magical; I was amazed by how he could play the violin so beautifully without eyesight. I used to close my eyes at home to see if I could do anything. It was hard to even walk. I concluded that he was definitely doing magic. There was also a fat, very well-dressed woman named Ghamar. She had beautiful short hair and played the tabla while she sang. She really made our days at school unforgettable, which was probably one of the happiest and best memories that I have. It was a dream come true to go to my father's school. It was also a dream for parents to register their kids at his school. I remember that his kindergarten was the only school with a driving service. My father had bought a large seated van, and hired a nice, kind, and chubby man called Habib to be the driver. He was in his fifties, and wore very thick glasses that he'd secure on his face with a black rubber band that he'd tighten himself, and it made him look a little silly. But his best quality was that he was very patient. He smiled no matter how much noise we made, which was the best part because at home we could never do that. We could show happiness here, so we wished that school could be open twenty-four hours.

The school had a tall, good-looking woman as a principal who always wore great clothing, hairdos, and makeup. She was very serious as every principal should be. The janitor was an old man with white hair and a beard, who was always sweeping quietly, as if he was swimming in his thoughts. The interesting part was that we could call each of our teachers and even the principal by their first name, which was unheard of back then, and even nowadays in Iran.

My father used to invite his entire staff to every family event, where the musicians sang, played music, and enlivened the party. My mother did not like that. Even though they treated my mother like a queen every time she visited the school, my mother didn't like any of the women working for my father, especially the principal. Everybody knew my father was not a cheater. He never even looked at any woman in the eyes. He was never interested in fooling around.

As he became more established in the school industry, another brilliant idea came to my father's mind. Since he loved reading and writing, he decided to publish his own magazine. My father's monthly magazine included news, poems, politics, games, puzzles, and his own articles, which were always published on the first page. In those days, there were not many magazines available, especially in Shiraz. He loved to share useful news and teach people how to live better lives through reading his magazine. People began to wait eagerly for the next issue of his magazine, just as they would wait keenly to get their children into my father's kindergarten. Our life was at a point that every person would dream of. Life was great.

The magazine and the kindergarten turned my father into an even bigger celebrity than he was before. It got to the point where the prime minister and the king of Iran would invite him to celebrations and even call him into meetings. He got busier every day and had less time for my mother. My father had become a big part of society, which was something he always dreamed of. Even though they never got along in the first place, she didn't like his absence. My mother never appreciated the power and success that my father brought home. She was a comparer. She was never happy with anything. There was just one part of it all that she liked, and that was when my father was invited to dinners and celebrations by politicians. Every new event brought a brighter smile on her face. And it seemed only that part of her life was a dream come true. I think she loved attending the parties very much because it was the best way to show off to her cousins, and keep her head up in the family. She would wear the trendiest of gowns, which were tailored specifically for her, and she'd pair the gowns with beautiful and unique jewelry sets. Since she had large feet, her heels were customized and handmade. She booked appointments at the most famous hair salons, and sometimes they would come to our house to fix her hair and do her makeup. My mother was unquestionably living like royalty, a life that every woman would love to have.

But of course, she never liked to be behind in life in any way, and my father was running ahead of her like a gazelle. Usually in a marriage you do not compare or try to compete with each other, but to my mother, she was lagging far behind. Instead of enjoying the successes in her life, she started to get jealous or maybe tired of my father's huge achievements. He was extremely successful. So, she had to do something, or she would lose in the competition between them, which was in her head. She started to make investment decisions for her lands to make them grow. She never took advice from anyone, and went wherever her desires took her. She started to sell properties to put the money toward building a mansion on one of her lands. Many valuable properties were sold over the years. The mansion was not built in a growing area, but was very far from the city. The city never grew in the direction of the mansion, making it in the middle of nowhere. The investment was just a waste. My father never interfered. He never told her right from wrong of anything because she would never listen anyway. The mansion made them resent each other more than ever.

—⚏—

Chapter 3

No matter where you are in the world, summer is something you look forward to. It is a relief from cold winters and rainy springs and the long school days, homework, and exams for all students. It's like a recharging season. You plug yourself into the calming heat, and repower your mental state of mind. To kids, summer means freedom, when you can play without limits, from morning to night. Summer for me meant gathering with family in my father's garden on Fridays, beside a beautiful water creek, feeling the cool breeze under tree shadows, and most of all seeing my mother laughing and talking. Mother never asked us to be quiet when we were in the garden.

Life on summer Fridays was like heaven for a short period of time. Of course, Aunt Mah was never allowed to join us. We always wished she could be there with us. One of our favorite things to do was to swim in the creek. Us kids played and played until we fell asleep like a group of dead dolls, and our parents probably had to carry us one by one into the house. Even though we were neighbors and played with our cousins every day, Fridays were something special.

During summers, life is less formal for adults as well. You see more happiness in them too. Kids understand every reaction that adults have, and nothing makes them happier than seeing their parents happy.

We also went on vacation every summer. The destination of our vacation always had a religious purpose to it. Our trip was always to Mashhad, a city in Iran, where many travel to visit the eighth Shia Imam's mausoleum, and pray for themselves and their families. Maybe you could say this pilgrimage was not a real vacation, but it was a getaway from home nonetheless. So we still got excited when our mother told us we were going to Mashhad. Our vacations weren't very luxurious because our mother and father wanted to save as much money as they could. Either way, the best part of the trip was that Mother loved it, felt happy, and spent time with us, and it was the only time when we had Father with us for every minute of the day. People usually drove to Mashhad from Shiraz, but my father never had the desire to drive, so he never got his license. That's why we didn't own a car and used buses or took the taxi or relatives' cars to go places. So every time we wanted to go to Mashhad, we took the bus, which took two days to get there. As a kid, it wasn't so bad; we actually loved the bus ride. We really made the most out of it. It was like going on a road trip with many other people who we'd become friends with, and every second of it passed by quickly with talking and singing.

When we arrived at our destination, we would find the cheapest and the most unwelcoming motels to stay in. The motels were really bad and unpleasant and very crowded with several types of people. Cheap motels anywhere else in the world are more luxurious than the ones we stayed in. They were so affordable that even homeless people would often check in to them. Our rooms didn't have bathrooms. There was always just one common bathroom that every motel guest had to share. A vacation should consist of pampering yourself and treating yourself with things you don't normally get at home but then again, what would my well-educated father know about vacation? We went days without a shower because we were afraid of the strangers down the halls. The other guests seemed too scary to share public showers with. I always wonder how my father trusted those places to take us there. He never worried about bad things happening to his children and his beautiful wife. He didn't really pay any attention to those kinds of details. Or maybe he didn't care. Either way, he saved money. I'm sure no one in the motel ever thought of the possibility that my family was wealthy. Believe me, after a week or two of living like that in those motels, we would forget that we were wealthy too. The fact that we looked poor never bothered us because we never felt any difference between us and others. It was the fact that we were among people that looked dangerous and kind of threatening that was the scary and worst part. As always, my siblings and I made the most out of it. We made lots of friends with the children present at the motels, and enjoyed our vacation as if we were in Paris.

When we got home from our vacation, we would spend most of our time in our yard because it was still summer and the weather was enjoyable and beautiful. Our yard was big, and covered with tiles. All the houses in Shiraz used to have cemented ponds. The ponds helped to store water to wash the tiles in the yard, to keep them clean and water the garden, or even wash clothes and dishes. Splashing water on the tiles made summer evenings much cooler. Around the wall, there were almost a hundred clay vases of geraniums. We knew that when the sun went down, we were supposed to fetch water with buckets and throw it on the yard's tiles. We loved doing it. In bigger houses like ours, there were several rooms beside the front door, which were used for servants. Since my mother didn't want to spend money on maids and it was her house, she rented the extra rooms to other families. A large family of eight to twelve lived in each of the rooms. All of them seemed very happy, much happier than we were. My aunts and uncle never had tenants. All of our tenants had access to our yard. Whenever we stepped outside, it was like going into a public park with so many people doing their own things. I can't complain because I was good friends with the tenants' children, and it was fun to play with them.

Smoking shisha is very common in Iran, especially back then. Shisha is an oriental tobacco pipe with a long flexible tube connected to a container, where the smoke is cooled by making it pass through water. Once you set up the shisha, you have to suck on the pipe a few times before the smoke is ready and perfect to be inhaled. My mother and father made me prepare it for them every time we were out in our yard. I had to smoke the tobacco a few times before it was ready for them to enjoy. I was only six. I grew up to become a smoker and have never been able to quit.

Just like any other season, summer ended, and a new school year began. That year I started going to grade one, and I was very excited. All those dreams of going to school, like Amene and Zein, and magically learning how to read and write would soon come true.

Chapter 4

THERE ARE SOME SET STAGES IN LIFE. BY STAGES, I MEAN the ages when you first go to school, then high school, then college, then get married, have kids, and live life by growing old with the love of your life. These stages shouldn't be lived all at once. Your age should be a ticket to each level, and each level is a goal to reach. Each level gets harder and harder, just like playing a video game. Some people give up or die easily in the game. But, I'm a fighter.

I was finally old enough to go to first grade. The thought and excitement of finally getting the chance to wear a cute uniform with white bows in my hair and walk to school with Amene, play in the schoolyard, and do homework kept me up all night. Going to school did not frighten me like some kids. Girls are born dreamers. But, our dreams change fast as new ones come and old ones disappear. When I was six, my only dream was going to a grade school.

When I was in first grade, my sister Amene was in fifth. She looked slightly older, but was short with a baby face. It was great to walk to school with her. I could feel safe and secure around her. Our ages were still close enough for us to understand each other. She was always a quiet and kind sister, whom I could rely on. Whenever my siblings and I played house, she was always the mom, and she was a wonderful mother. She cooked imaginary foods for us, and told us all the great stories that she read in school. She let us talk, and never told us to be quiet.

Months passed by, and we were enjoying every moment of the school days. We were always busy with homework, and I was so proud of learning the alphabet. For each word, I learned to write or read, I got super excited, as if I had discovered a new star in the sky.

One day when we got home from school, my father was home. This was very peculiar since he never came home until late except for Fridays. Seeing my parents not arguing and sitting calmly meant something was up. I was a curious child. I wanted to know why he was home, but simply asking would not give me the right answer, and so I had to eavesdrop. I started listening to their conversation, and investigated to see what they were up to. I saw lots of fruits and empty dirty dishes, tea cups and some fresh pastry, so for sure they had guests, but why at that time of the day? Why when we were not at home?

And then I heard it. I was right. There was a serious problem. My mother and father were getting Amene married. She was just ten years old. She was just a confused little girl whose only concern should be homework. Not marriage, not a husband. The thought of marriage at this age was frightening. She was still at an age when she needed to be with her mother and siblings. I told myself for sure I had heard something wrong, because that big news should have been told to her directly. I stopped trying to figure it out. I was afraid that I was correct about Amene getting married, and hoped that I was making a silly mistake. No parent would do that. Especially a mother who herself had suffered because of an arranged marriage at the age of fourteen. Our cousins were the same age as us, and they lived like normal kids, and no one dared to even suggest to our uncle and aunts for their daughters' hands in marriage. We only saw it in movies that were based on a hundred years ago, when fathers married off their daughters for money. We once saw a movie in which they traded their daughter for a sack of rice. But we were not poor. I went back to thinking positively, and tried to forget about my suspicion. Days passed, and everything seemed fine, and I even got to a point where I had forgotten all about it. And that is when my mother called Amene over.

Amene looked into my eyes with worry, like she knew, all this time, but never mentioned it. Perhaps she wished that it was all just a bad dream, and that she had heard it wrong too. I squeezed her hands and did not let go. I followed her into the kitchen, where my mother was waiting for her. I kept telling Amene that everything would be fine. I stretched the fake smile on my face as wide as I could, so that she would feel calm and okay. But my heart was pounding loudly, and I had a feeling that I was right all along. Being right never felt so wrong. My mother told me to leave, but I did not. She ignored me. She excitedly told Amene that by the end of the fifth grade a handsome man would be waiting to marry her.

Amene's tears burst out like a volcano. "So for real, you are selling me? Are you trading me?" she asked between sobs. Please, please, please do not do this to me," she bawled over and over again.

My mother stood there looking at her. "You are just a child. You do not know what is best for you. Parents know what is right for their kids." My mother smiled as if everything was fine, and I wished I could sense sincerity in her voice, but I really did not. All I sensed was fake compassion that was more bogus than my smile. I began to cry, I cried for Amene. And Amene cried like a child who had lost a doll or had not completed her homework. What if they made me marry too? I thought to myself. My sister cleverly began to reason with my mother. "Can I do anything to change your mind? I will help more at home. I will wash the dishes for the rest of my life. Can we make a deal? If I get extremely good grades by the end of this year, can I continue school and not marry? But if I get bad grades, then you have my word, I will marry any man you put my way."

For some reason, my mother accepted the deal. Maybe she did it just to get rid of us, and stop us from crying. Or, she may have thought through her stupid decision to force her child to marry a man. She promised Amene that she would not make her marry if she did better at school and got good grades.

From that day on, everything about Amene was different. She was quieter, and did not smile at all. She ate very little. She looked pale, and was scared. Even on our walks to school, Amene would never say a word. Until the end of grade five, my sister studied as if her life depended on it. And it really did.

I helped her as much as a first grader could. I sat close to her wherever she went and said nothing. She was too sad to talk. I brought her food as she studied, and I prayed for her. I prayed that God would give her so much intelligence that she would ace every test, and run away from the cage my mother and father were going to lock her in. But I couldn't find much hope in her eyes. I guess she knew how our parents were. She had probably figured out how selfish and careless they were. How could she trust my mother's promise? Either way, she owed it to herself to try as hard as she could.

I stopped enjoying my first-grade dreams, and just went to school like it was a chore. The school year was coming to its end, and Amene studied hard for her exams.

It was time. The report cards came in. When I received my own, I did not even open it. I was only eager to see Amene's marks. I ran to find her, and there she was with her old smile back on her pale round face. That was the biggest smile I had seen on her in a long time. "I did it," she said. We cried tears of joy, held hands, and jumped up and down like the little schoolgirls that we were. It was a pure relief. We ran and danced our way home. We told my mother with pride and happiness. When Amene showed my mother her grades, my mother stayed expressionless. "Good job," she said, "Now I have news as well."

That's when we got disappointed with my mother. Her *news* was not good. We knew this for sure. It was words that made Amene grind her teeth and want to scream. Her *news* was that she had planned Amene's wedding, and that everything was arranged and ready to go. All those months of Amene's silence and sadness did not change anything; they knew they were going to force her to marry the entire time. "But what about our deal?" Amene's eyes watered. Her voice was soft and hopeless. "It is great that you got good grades," my mother said. "But girls should get married and have kids and create a beautiful life…and now is a good time to get married," she continued. My mother's smile was the sourest smile that I had ever seen; her eyes were glowing in a scary way, her heart screamed emptiness, and her teeth were laughing. It seemed like she thought she had cracked a joke and expected everyone to laugh. But she wasn't funny. She wasn't cracking jokes. She was only saying horrendous and unfair words.

"But I am just a child. What do I know about marriage? I just finished grade five. I have a long way to go to finish my education." Amene sighed. But my mother said she did not feel like arguing, and that the decisions had been made anyway. She added, "I went to school until grade six and I can easily read and write, but that changed nothing in my life as a housewife. You do not need a high school diploma to wash dishes and raise a child. You are just a little girl who does not understand." Then she yelled, as if she was tired of the conversation, "Now go on and play with your sisters. It has been a long day for me and I do not have the energy to bargain." My mother was right that Amene was supposed to play.

"What can we do about it?" I asked her.

"Nothing," she responded and cried louder.

Amene began to change. She did not cry anymore, nor did she complain. What could a child do when her parents forced her to do things? She was silent, and did as she was told. It was as if my mother and father had sucked the soul out of her, and tied strings to her arms and legs, and ordered her around like an uninspired puppet. My sister no longer smiled the beautiful smile that I had seen on the day she got her report card. She was drowned somewhere deep in her sorrows. She refused to look directly into my mother's eyes, the woman who had betrayed her. My sister felt like an innocent person who was going to be executed. She had no power to defend herself; there was only a weak body that was pushed around unfairly by selfish adults. "God help Amene!" That was all I could come up with during those long, sad days.

My parents kept the marriage proposal and the wedding planning a secret from the rest of my family, even my uncle and aunts. Maybe they knew how stupid and childish it would be for a reputable, well-educated man to marry off his ten-year-old daughter. When my uncle finally found out, he was devastated that my mother and father were doing this to Amene. I heard him yelling at my mother, "How could you ever even let yourselves hand an innocent child to a grown man?!" He pressed his forehead against his palm nervously. "What is this? Have we traveled three hundred years ago back in time? This is child abuse." He was sweating, and walking fast in circles as if he were going out of his mind. "This is a crime and should be illegal. I should put you two in jail." He started begging my mother to let Amene live a normal kid's life. "If you do not want her I will take care of her with pleasure, but please change your minds. For God's sake, what is wrong with you people? Why do you always like to cause trouble?!" he shouted.

My mother kept saying it was my father's decision, and that she did not like to argue with Father, as if their entire marriage didn't consist of arguing. "It is hard to believe that you cannot do anything about this! Shame on you both." His face turned purple as he screamed at Mother and walked out of the house. It was true. My deranged father was behind all of this. It was all him. His religious mind convinced him that child marriage was a right thing to do. But it was done some fourteen hundred years ago, when they used to marry off young girls to solve problems between tribes and prevent war. Not now. Not in this day and age. My mother always argued and disagreed with my father for every single thing in life. But she agreed to this one thing that affected her daughter. It was very hard for everyone in the family to believe that my mother could not stand in the way of this. She just didn't care enough because it did not affect her; it affected Amene. Otherwise, she would have fought hard, broke dishes, and thrown shoes and pots and pans at my father until he changed his mind. But she kept quiet and contributed to ruining Amene's childhood. I often heard her gloating about becoming the youngest mother-in-law in the family. Of course, to her, it was always about being number one in everything. She didn't realize they would call her the number one idiot and child abuser and the worst mother in the family.

The legal age for marriage was fourteen at that time, but this didn't stop my mother and father. The groom's family agreed not to get a marriage certificate until Amene turned fourteen.

It was time for Amene to meet her future husband at their engagement party. It was going to be the first time that she would face her destiny. She didn't have a choice. Ugly or handsome, kind or abusive, healthy or not, that was it. At the engagement party, my sister and I found out that the groom's name was Hadi, and he was twenty-seven years old, the same age as my mother. Amene was only ten. I wonder if my parents thought of the future or not. For example, in twenty years when Amene was thirty her husband would be forty-seven, and when she was in her fifties, he would be an old man. Hadi was tall and broad-shouldered and came from a very rich, well-known family in Shiraz. He was always dressed in suits, and had nice and shiny black hair. They were textile merchants and owned many properties. The groom lost his father when he was ten and had been working hard for the family business ever since. He lived with his mother and two younger brothers. The other brothers and sisters were married and went their own ways, and now it was his turn. They got engaged, and in the spring they got married before Amene even finished grade six.

Who can hear a child's voice if not her own parents? Where was God when Amene shouted with her eyes and cried in silence?

After the wedding, all the respect that my family had for my mother and father was lost. Most of the family judged from afar, but stayed out of it because they felt like it was none of their business. And the people who tried to stop it, like my uncle, couldn't manage to change my parents' minds. They all had a "You're on your own now" attitude toward my parents. My parents never noticed that people were looking down on them for what they had just done, or maybe they didn't *want* to notice, or they didn't care at all. Their heads were held high as if they had just done the greatest thing. As if they'd accomplished something. They were very proud of having Hadi's family being added to our family.

Amene was sent to live with Hadi and her mother-in-law after the wedding. Hadi's mother was as controlling as our mother. She was very religious and immediately forced Amene to wear a complete hijab, which was the chador. Amene was not allowed to visit us on her own free will. She had to seek permission for that. The first time she was allowed to come see us, my mother had to invite Hadi's family over for a formal dinner. It was unusual to see my mother cleaning the house. She was suddenly obsessed with making everything perfect for Hadi and his mother. She made everyone wear their best clothes, and instructed us to be on our best behavior. We had to be very formal. We never had a conversation or shared any laughs with Amene's husband. We had to be very polite and quiet and serious with him. We never called him by his first name. If we had to, we would call him by his last name including the title Mmister. He was not a bad person, but he did not have a friendly face or attitude, and he mostly looked angry and serious. The worst part was that my siblings and I were not even allowed to talk to Amene. I never understood why my mother cared so much when she found out that Amene was going to visit because she was the one who kicked her out. Amene's visit was very short. After a couple of hours, they left, and no one knew when she would get the permission from her prison guard to visit her family again. No one knew how she felt in her new house, and what was going on deep down in her mind and heart. From what I saw, she looked startled and empty, as if she had transformed into a robot. Looking at Amene's face, you would be ashamed as a father and mother to think about what you had done.

—⁂—

Chapter 5

AMENE WAS DEAD INSIDE. SHE WAS JUST EXISTING, A shell of a girl. She could've been a child longer, but was forced to be a woman. As her soul couldn't catch up, it started to fade instead. My mother and father created an unnecessary lifetime problem for her. But it was preventable, just a scarring human error.

When Amene was gone, a part of me went missing too. She was the star of my soul, which had died. I began to adapt to the fact that Amene was no longer my playmate and my best friend. She had a new life, and it was not going to be easy for me if I did not let go of her and move on. I had to accept all the wrong facts. Of course, for my parents everything was normal from the very first day. Nothing made them worry around Amene's quiet and sad personality. And whenever someone mentioned it or was concerned, they would just say that one day she would get used to it and would realize how we only wanted the best for her. At least life went on great for my parents, and probably that was all that mattered to them. My new star was my younger sister Masume. Now that she was old enough to go to school, we would walk together just like Amene and I used to. And this is how I really got to bond with her. Something about Masume really brightened up my day. Her personality shined very brightly. We had so much in common. We'd laugh all the way to school and buy snacks with our allowances. The friendship and sisterhood I built with Masume really helped me to feel better. But there would always be moments where Amene's profoundly sad face flashed in my memory and made me sad. We were three sisters who were always close, and nothing could make me forget that. The three of us not only cared for one another, but we also really cared about other people. If any of our schoolmates told us a sad story about their lives, we would cry with them in sympathy. Most of the time we would also give our daily allowances to some of the in-need kids. My mother hardly cried and even if she did, tears never came out of her eyes. It was just a dry way of crying. She did not have generous hands either. She was never really charitable like the other members of our family, like my aunts. Perhaps we felt empathy and learned to give from our aunts. Thank God, because I like to help people...even if it sometimes hurts me.

One day, as Masume and I were walking to school, we saw a little boy sitting in the middle of the way and crying out loud. As I was a very nosy kid, we stopped and asked him what had happened. He pointed to a bowl of yogurt and said that his stepmother gave him money to buy yogurt and it fell out of his hands. "I cannot go back home without yogurt because she will beat me with a belt," he sobbed. We comforted him and bought yogurt with our allowances and gave it to him. That made him very happy. He held the bowl very close to his chest as if his life depended on it and went back home. We liked adventure, and helping made us feel very good. Anytime we went back home and told these stories to my mother, she said, "You girls are crazy. If you are too kind in this world, you will never be happy. You will always be concerned about something or someone. You cannot help everyone in this world, so you should let it go. God will help whoever he wants."

Maybe she was right that we would never be able to help everybody, but for those few people who we comforted *were* the world to us. Maybe if everybody in the world was kind enough to help just a little, everybody's problems would get solved. Our mother couldn't change us. We never overlooked any person who needed help. Big or small, we tried our best to help.

I knew that one day we were going to move on with our lives too, just like Amene did. But I wished it would not be anytime soon because the times I shared with Masume became the best times of my life, which turned into great memories that still make me smile when I reminisce about them. I wish all memories could be as delightful as helping others, playing games, going to school, and laughing without a care in the world. But life is not a fairy tale. It's always been more serious than my little dreams.

I remember the times when we would count our steps to school and hop over cracks on the sidewalk. We would shoot stones or cans at each other that were lying around on the asphalt with the tip of our shoes. We would laugh until tears came out of our eyes. I remember having a classmate named Sima, who was very skinny compared to all of us. She was always quiet and sad because her parents never got along, and she was afraid that they would separate. Back then rarely would anyone get divorced. The law dictated that if a woman wanted a divorce, she wouldn't get custody of her children. So women usually suffered through their marriages, wasting their youth by living with the wrong man just so that they could be with their children. One day, Sima was crying because her mother had left home and wanted to divorce her father. I told her not to worry and that I would talk to my mother, hoping that she could do something about it since we knew her family. My promise made her face glow and smile again. When I went home, I immediately talked to my mother about Sima's situation. The best part of my mother's attitude was that she really cared about bringing couples back together. She had done it before, and I liked that about her. She did not refuse to help, and dressed up immediately to go to Sima's house. My mother talked to Sima's father and convinced him respectfully that he needed his wife, and that his life would be so much easier if his wife came back home peacefully. He seemed like a kind man with a wrong attitude. My mother even volunteered to go with him to his in-laws' home, so they could see that he was willing to change. That same night, my parents and siblings and I went to Sima's grandmother's house. And just like that, Sima's life went back to normal for as long as I knew them.

One day when Amene came to visit, she looked much chubbier than before. Little did I know that she was pregnant! Masume and I got very excited when we found out that we were going to be aunts. It made us feel like we were all grown-ups. The hardest part was the months before we got to see our niece or nephew. My mother was excited as much as we were, and she kept reminding us to be patient because those months would be worth the wait in the end. I guess we all forgot the fact that Amene was going to be a fourteen-year-old mom. But nothing was going to change that, so we chose to enjoy it.

Finally, all the waiting came to an end and the day arrived. My very own sister gave birth at the age of fourteen to the most stunning baby boy. He was named Mohammad. He was very special and beautiful. Mohammad was born with light hazel eyes and light brown hair. He was so chubby and innocent that I swear I could eat him up.

Masume and I attacked Mohammad with love and kisses every time we saw him. Amene giggled as we all huddled over Mohammad and sang to him. We all looked at one another and sang louder and louder, holding Mohammad up in the air. He was very quiet and let us handle him in any way that we wanted, just like a doll. Gazing at his hazel-brown eyes was like looking at a planet in outer space. He brought so much sunshine in our days that the attention was all on him no matter who surrounded us. After her pregnancy, Amene came back to life. We could see a bit of happiness in her eyes that we hadn't seen in the past four years. Maybe she started to accept her life the way it was.

"He's really nice to me, you know," Amene quietly told Masume and me once after dinner. "It's really his mother that's... She's okay. No, well. He's nice." She couldn't find her words, but it was the first time that I was hearing anything about her marriage. You could feel that she had decided to just look ahead and never look back. She believed, after four years, it was better to feel like an adult than to suffer being a prisoner in her childhood, which was unfairly stolen from her. She never talked about her problems because that was something my mother had taught us. Even as kids we never opened up to my mother, and so what was the point of complaining when Amene knew that my mother could not change anything. "He treats me well, especially now, with Mohammad." Hadi's kindness made her accept her life the way it was. But mostly, we could tell how she felt just by the way she carried herself. She started to speak more when she visited us, and no one stopped her. We still weren't allowed to build too much of a relationship with Amene, but Mohammad became a great excuse for Masume and me to sit with Amene and talk to her. Becoming a mother gave her new hope and light for the future, even though she knew she was just a young girl and should be at school studying. After four long years of grayness, we put the past behind us and were just enjoying the company of our new family member.

Slowly, Amene was allowed to visit us more often. She was even allowed to come early on Friday mornings when schools were closed and stay all day until her husband came for dinner, and then they would leave together. We could play with Mohammad until the last minute that they were with us. On a Friday, as I held Mohammad while Masume kissed his cheeks, Amene was just looking at us and smiling for a long time. Amene said, "Mohammad loves his aunts, just look at him. He never cries when you hold him." She got up and sat closer to me, and put her hand on my leg while she looked into my eyes. "I love you, Najma, and you, Masume, and Mohammad, my son, my brothers...and I love coming here, seeing you guys, and being with you all." I felt warm. I hadn't heard that from her in years. I felt my sister return from the days that we used to walk to school together. I felt the bond that I had with her revive suddenly. Amene was happy. She was enjoying her son and her new freedom. Her mother-in-law was a little easier on her and my mother didn't stop us from talking to her, which brought a lot of life back into Amene. She needed us, and she was finally allowed to have us. Everything was going well. Perhaps happiness was coming back into our family.

Chapter 6

Time passed in the blink of an eye, and I turned eleven. As Mohammad grew older and more time passed in Amene's marriage, I realized how much her life had shattered. Maybe she looked happy now, but I knew that she forced herself to be happy. If you looked at her a little longer when she smiled, you'd notice her smile faded quickly. As if it was forced, and wasn't genuine. Like a clown with the happy, bright clothes and makeup who always smiled, but was he really happy behind that mask? What else could she do?

Things started to get strange in our house again. My father started coming home earlier on his work days, and my mother was always making phone calls and speaking quietly. A strange woman that I had never seen before kept visiting my mother for tea and sweets, and we were never allowed to join them. I wasn't that curious. Ever since Amene left, I focused more on my relationship with my siblings than my mother and father. There was a trust I once had in my mother and father that began to fade over time as I witnessed what they did to Amene. But I still loved them. I was a child. I needed my parents. But I felt like their roles were different from what I had imagined. So I stopped imagining. For that same reason, I stopped wondering what they were up to in their lives, just as they did not wonder what was going on in mine.

It was a Friday afternoon when my mother and father were smoking shisha in our yard. Masume and I were playing catch with the tenant children. "Come on, Najma, throw it over here!" Masume called out. The sun was shining bright and I couldn't see where the ball was every time that it was in the air. "I'm throwing it at you, Najma! You ready?!" yelled one of the boys. "Ready!" I yelled back. The ball went way past my head and landed somewhere behind my mother and father. They didn't notice it. I ran toward the ball, and just as I went to pick it up, I heard, "You should've seen her. You really should've," my mother said. "You know I don't care what she looked like. Come on. Were they well-off?" My father seemed a bit frustrated. "Were they well-off?" my mother mocked him. "Of course, they were. No one not well-off would have had the audacity to ask for our daughter's hand. Are you kidding me?" My mother smoked in distress. "I like them. I think they're the one."

"Bring the ball over already!" Masume yelled. I snapped back into reality. I threw her the ball and went inside. And then it occurred to me. I was the oldest daughter in the house. I was eleven. And I was next. It was in that moment of realization that I was silenced. We have a saying in Shiraz: when a mule falls into a pothole once, he would never step into it again. Even mules knew better than my parents.

It wasn't long after that, when my parents finally told me in person. My mother went on and on about how it was time for me to take on the responsibility of being a woman, and how exciting this was going to be for me. "Okay," I responded. I didn't have the fight in me. I fought for Amene. And Amene fought for herself. But there was no result. There was no bright outcome. There was simply no point. This wasn't a choice; I wasn't being *asked* if I wanted to get married. I was being *told* that I would be getting married. I wasn't confused. I knew what was happening to my life, and I was just silenced. I was quiet. I was weak. I had dreams just like every other child, but my mother and father built a brick wall in front of me and stopped me from moving forward, stopped my thoughts from moving forward. This moment, I felt, was the moment I stopped living the life that I had wanted to live. I was stuck here. An eleven-year-old girl was stuck. My soul stayed right in place while the rest of me, just a shell of my body, continued for the rest of my life.

During her next visit, I told Amene what had happened. "I'll talk to Mother and Father, Najma. Don't worry." It was worth a try, but I had no hope. I didn't fantasize about Amene magically solving this problem. But I didn't stop her. "What are you going to say?" I asked. "Don't worry about that." When the time was right, she talked to them privately. She may have explained how hard and unfair her life was as a young wife and mother. Maybe she told them that I could do so much more with my life, if I could just continue school and focus on myself. I don't know what she said, but I know that she tried her best for me. But still my parents did not care. My parents always said the same thing over and over: "You're young, and you don't know what's best for you. We know what's best for you. One day you'll realize it."

When my uncle found out, he tried harder to stop my parents from marrying me off than he did for Amene. But of course, his efforts didn't achieve any results. No one could change my parents' minds. And no one really understood why my parents were so adamant about doing this. For a woman who had never been happy with her marriage, I thought my mother would understand. But she did not.

On the morning of my wedding day, I was shown my dress. It was really pretty. It was custom designed and handmade by a tailor. It looked like the expensive types of gowns that my mother wore to her big important parties. I guess it was meant to make me feel beautiful, but it only made me feel like a little girl in women's clothing. My mother–in-law booked the best salon in Shiraz for my hair and makeup. All the expenses were paid by my in-laws.

The salon was reserved just for me. "Wow, you have beautiful, strong hair." A young woman with red hair and thick eyeliner approached me. "You must be Najma, you stunning girl. Let's get started." She did my hair just like

Cinderella's. She put more makeup on me than I had ever seen on my mother. They wanted my makeup to make me look older— more like a woman. When my hair and makeup were done, my mother gave me my dress to wear. I slipped into heels for the first time. They made me taller, but I still felt small. "You're all set! Here, look in this mirror. See what you look like!" My hairdresser was excited about what she had done. I looked in the mirror and saw a broken girl with too much makeup on, in glamorous clothes. Everything made me feel so small. I looked ridiculous. There was a pressure in my chest ever since I found out that I was getting married. Now that I looked in the mirror, the pressure felt unbearable. Even all the glamour couldn't fill up my emptiness.

"They'll be here any minute! Don't eat anything. You need to look good." My mother was frantic and energetic while I was quiet and tired. It was my wedding day. I always imagined falling in love like Scarlett and Rhett in *Gone with the Wind*, but that could no longer be. My soon-to-be husband was going to pick me up along with his mother and his sisters-in-law, to take me to his home for my wedding. This was going to be the first time that I was going to meet him. I didn't know what to do when they arrived. I didn't really know what to expect. I just knew his name was Hassan. "Najma and Hassan, Najma and Hassan, Hassan and Najma." I kept repeating our names in my head to see if it would calm me. It didn't. I felt anxious. It didn't click. It wasn't right. I wasn't supposed to know the name of the man that I was going to marry before I'd even seen him. I was supposed to look at a man in the crowd and be awestruck. I was supposed to wonder who this man was, and hope he'd notice me, and come over and say hello. I was supposed to daydream about how handsome and perfect he was, and *then* I'd find out his name. First, there would be chemistry, and then we would fall in love, and would find out about each other's interests through many conversations and moments of my wishing he'd ask me to marry him.

And *then* we'd get married. But that didn't happen. I knew his name. His face didn't matter. His presence in a crowd didn't matter. Our chemistry didn't matter. There was no chance to fall in love and daydream. All of that was cut out of the timeline by my mother and father, and I was left with a wedding day devoid of any magic.

"Don't stop smiling. Did you hear me?" My mother snapped me back to reality. "And don't talk too much. Now go on. They're outside." I couldn't move for a moment. I was frozen. "Go on now! Go, go. Have fun and don't forget to smile." A blue-and-white Opel was parked in front of our house. It was Hassan's car. I walked toward the car and suddenly the doors opened, and everybody stepped out. There was a woman in a chador along with four beautiful other women. And then there was him. He was taller than my father, and handsomer. His eyes were large and an inviting brown in shade. His hair was dark and combed neatly. He had a tailored casual suit on, which matched his eyes perfectly along with shoes that looked brand-new. But he was twenty-four, a university student studying mechanical engineering. I was eleven. I was still afraid; I wanted to go back to my house. "Hello, my child. How beautiful you are. I'm Hassan's mother. You can call me Bibi. Oh, just look at your beauty." Her smile was warm. She looked into my eyes and I felt her honesty. But my heart was beating fast, and I couldn't even breathe. "Hi." I smiled just as I was told. Hassan had lost his father when he was eighteen. He had died from a typhoid fever, which had spread in Iran and killed thousands of people. I was told that his father was a very kind and generous merchant who was very well-known in the city and loved his wife. Hassan had four brothers and no sisters. His mother was a very important member in his family, and was very well respected all around. She was fat and short with long gray hair, which was always braided and lay on her shoulders. She had a pointy nose and very kind eyes. Hassan's brothers were all married and had kids. I was the same age as some of Hassan's nieces and nephews. Hassan was the youngest son. He loved his mother more than any of his other brothers, and she loved him very much too, as he was the kindest to her. "Come, meet your *jaaris*." Bibi introduced me to Hassan's sisters-in-law. There were four, one for each of his brothers. They were nice too. But my mind was in a haze. I couldn't think straight. I felt like people were speaking to me, but all I could hear was words that seemed to be coming from miles away. "I'm Hassan." He didn't say much, but he smiled a little. Before I could collect my thoughts, I was in the backseat of the Opel with strangers, headed to their home.

When we got back to their house, everything was set up and ready for the party. My mind was blank. I felt overwhelmed by all the changes. I was surrounded by strangers and stranger things. There were musicians setting up their instruments, and tables full of pastries, fruits, and desserts. On one big table there was nothing but a several-tier cake that a lady was touching up. There it was: my wedding cake. It was white and detailed. I didn't crave it. I didn't want it. It was supposed to be celebratory, but I didn't want to celebrate. I didn't want music or sweets or any of what was going on around me. I was terrified. I didn't know anybody, and everybody was working hard for my night. This wasn't *my* night; it was my mother and father's. I felt like a guest. "Look at the dessert table; I'm sure everybody will find something they like on it." Bibi came up behind me. My stomach was tied up in a knot, and nothing looked good to me. "Thank you." I felt sick. I smiled like mother told me to.

The guests began to arrive. And in the blink of an eye, the home was filled with hundreds of people. It was a two-story mansion with more rooms than I could count. The party was mainly held in the huge backyard, which they had filled with colored lights that hung everywhere. Hundreds of chairs were lined up side by side the entire length of the backyard. All kinds of flowers were on the tables, along the pathways on the floor, and hanging from the trees. They were literally everywhere. The colored lights reflected off the flowers and made them look more exotic. There was a small table in front of every four chairs, full of sweets and fruits. Many waiters were walking around and constantly serving tea from nice trays. Serving tea is a way to show respect to guests in Iran, and the more you serve them tea, the more they will appreciate your party. The dinner table was massive. It had a ridiculous amount of choices. There were all kinds of meats, poultry, and seafood. There were different types of rice, stews, and salads. The table was set beautifully, and everything smelled so good. There was enough food to feed the whole town. Everything around me was beautiful. But I felt like I was looking for the bride and the groom. It wasn't me. It wasn't supposed to be me.

Because my father had a magazine business, he got photographers who worked for his magazine to take professional pictures of our wedding. Having a photographer for a wedding was very expensive because pictures were very rare and so were the photographers. Not many weddings had them. It was tradition that the groom's family covered all the wedding expenses. I wished the wedding was my parents' responsibility. That way maybe they wouldn't marry us off because of the expenses, as they were misers.

I was limping and tumbling everywhere. The heels were difficult to walk in, but I didn't want to look funny. I felt my face sweating; it felt heavy with all the makeup. Nothing was going well. I turned around and there they were, my mother and father, Zein, and Masume. I looked around in the crowds and I saw Hadi and Mohammad. My eyes locked with Amene's. She started to walk toward me. "You look beautiful," Amene said with her kind smile. Masume agreed and held my hand. "We love you, Najma." I began to tear up. I felt all my emotions catch up to me. "No, sis. There will be none of that tonight. We're here for you." Amene was being strong for me.

I could feel it. I group hugged my sisters. I noticed that my mother and father were long gone. They were mingling with the guests, barely looking at me. Every time I looked at my mother, she was laughing.

Hassan suddenly came up to me. He wasn't smiling. He looked worried and afraid, like a mirror image of all the things that I felt inside. He held out his hand. I could hear myself gulp. I just stared at it, standing still, breathing uneasy. He looked at me as if he knew that I had a thousand thoughts rushing through my head. He could see that I was frightened and wanted to go home. I wanted to be a kid. He could see it. All I could think about was how much older than me he was. He could've found a girl at the university, someone who matched with him more in age and intellectuality. I wondered if he had offered his hand to other women. If he had been forced into this marriage the way I was. I stared at his outstretched hand and felt afraid and alone. "Don't worry; I've never held another girl's hand either," he said gently, as if he read my mind. That was all that he ever said to me that whole night. We just held hands in silence. It felt foreign and strange. My hand was shaky. I felt the warmth of my hand travel to his. We were touching, and yet I felt so distant and lonely. I had a feeling that he was forced to marry me too. There was kindness in his eyes and he kept stealing quick glances at me. I didn't know if he was just a quiet person or if he had secrets. Maybe he was thinking about his father not being there on his wedding night.

I knew that he felt sorry for me, and somewhere deep down, I felt sorry for him too. When the night was almost over, I looked in the crowd and saw Masume. I looked into her eyes and silently said goodbye to our adventures and great times that we had had together. And while I sat with Hassan, hand in hand, I mourned my childhood.

Chapter 7

The last of the guests left. The wedding was officially over. Everything seemed so dark and blurry that I wanted my mother, I wanted my father. But they did not want me. I was so scared and hopeless that it felt hard to breathe. I wanted to go home. It was hard to see my family going home without me. I felt lost. "Did you have fun?" Bibi put her hand on my shoulder. I nodded. I couldn't speak. "Good. I'm glad. Okay, honey, Hassan will show you to your room, it's all set up and ready. It's just up the stairs." I was exhausted, but I didn't feel like sleeping. I was excited to be alone. I wanted to crawl up into a corner and embrace the quietness and the darkness. I needed to find myself again. "This is it." Hassan brought me to a large room with a big bed. He gestured for me to go inside. "Thank you," I mumbled. I couldn't wait until he left so that I could burst out crying. But he didn't leave. He came in. This wasn't my room. It was *our* room. "Get on the bed." His voice was firmer than it was during the party. I was scared. I couldn't hold back my tears anymore, and I started to cry. "Stop that!" he said with a little anger. He terrified me. I got on the bed and didn't make a sound. Tears were still streaming down my face, but I said nothing. He climbed on to the bed and made me lie down on my stomach. I buried my face in the pillow and screamed silently in my head as he raped me. It hurt me, both physically and mentally. My heart shattered with every thrust. My childhood was stolen, and dreams broken. I died a little that night. I felt betrayed by everyone. I thought he understood my being frightened. I thought he felt my pain when we were getting married. I thought his silence was kind and innocent. I thought he was shy and gentle. For a moment when we held hands in silence, I felt sorry for him. I thought he was trapped the way that I was. I was disgusted with myself for feeling that way as he raped me. I was disgusted by him. I was disgusted with my mother and father who put me here and trapped me with a stranger. A stranger was touching me, violating me, disrespecting me. And my parents were okay with it. I could never forget it. In that moment, I realized what Amene really went through and why she was so quiet for four years. I had no say in this. I was nothing. I felt dirty and worthless.

This became a routine. Every night I surrendered my body to him and he broke it. He broke me, bit by bit each and every night. I tried to remember who I was; I wanted something to hold on to. I wanted something in my control. Before my mother left for home after the wedding, she gave me a little advice. She looked at me sternly and said, "Always dress up. Look neat and clean and go down the stairs with a smile. Always, always smile. Remember to be polite and never talk to anybody about personal things in our family. If anybody asks you any questions, just say you don't know. Never talk back. Be quiet and do anything that you're asked." She taught me how to break on the inside, but look good on the outside. And that's all that she left me with. That's the only advice I had to hold on to, so I did. I smiled every morning, and didn't say anything at night.

That summer after the wedding, we were invited to parties. It was the tradition for close relatives to invite the bride and groom and their entire family over to celebrate. In the first month of marriage, I realized Hassan did not like to go to parties or be with people whom he did not know well. He would get so angry for every invitation from my side of the family. "I'm not coming to these events!" Hassan yelled at me. "You have to, darling." Bibi would gently convince him to go. He'd walk out with anger and stop talking to me. Then he'd show up to my family's events and not speak to anybody. He'd just say hi, thank you, and bye. I realized that was the reason for his quietness at our wedding. He wasn't shy; he just hated being there. And for a few days after each party, he would ignore me in front of his family and that made me embarrassed and sad, as I did not have anybody but him in that crowd. I was not even supposed to play with the kids because I had to act like an adult. He made me feel so alone. It was the same thing over and over again, every time somebody from my side of the family invited us to an event. One time, after my mother had already thrown a party after our wedding celebration, she invited only Hassan and me to come over for lunch. I had never seen Hassan so angry before that. "Why didn't your mother invite my whole family again?!" He took me to our room and shut the door behind him. "Your mother disrespected my family!" He put his hands around my neck and pulled me up. Then he threw me down and yelled, "Every time your family wants to see you, they have to invite every person in my family, all my brothers and their wives, their children, and my mother!" He charged closer to me and grabbed me by my neck again and pushed me against the wall. "Do you understand?!" He kept slapping and kicking me and repeating, "Do you understand!?" louder and louder. When he was done, he just straightened out his shirt and left the room. He closed the door quietly behind him. I lay on my side of the bed and stared at the floor. Tears were gently rolling down my cheek, which hit the rug that the bed sat on. My flesh felt tender and my mind went numb. I was raped every night and beaten every day. Every bone in my body ached, but nothing hurt more than my heart.

I didn't know what to do. I didn't know if I should tell my mother or Hassan's mother, or anybody at all. I was so afraid of him. I thought that if I told anyone, he would hit me more and I'd lose my prestige in front of others. I had my pride. But it was all shattered. I walked out of our room with a broken heart. I didn't want to be pitied and felt like no one could really help me, so I decided to never tell a single soul about how Hassan abused me. I had no safe haven to turn to. My own room was the scariest place in the house. I never wanted to be invited to my parents' house. My mother threw me out and even her invitations hurt me. At first, I thought Hassan was normal. I thought maybe all men were like this to their wives. Then I remembered my uncle, and my aunt Roohi and her husband, and Scarlett and Rhett. Then I thought, Well, nobody knows what happens behind closed doors. Maybe all husbands were really like Hassan. But it wasn't normal. Hassan had a dark, grim, petrifying side. *Dear Mother and Father, you destroyed my life. I am married to a monster*, I once wrote on a note, which I thought for a second I would give to my parents, but I ripped it apart as soon as I wrote it.

When it came to his own family events, he was a completely different person. He was funny and charming, truly the life of the party. Everybody loved him and wanted to be around him. He smiled and laughed. He'd look at me from time to time. He really looked like he was having fun. I didn't know how to deal with a man with a dark heart. A man with a hundred masks.

Hassan never talked to me about himself. He barely spoke to me. Bibi told me that he taught mechanics to high school students, as he was getting his mechanical engineering degree.

Now that it was summer he was on his holidays. We got married a few months before the schools started their new term. And now that summer was at its end, it was almost time for him to go back to work and his studies.

During Hassan's summer break, I wasn't allowed to go to my parents' house. I wasn't even allowed to leave his house. Every single day he would leave me alone with his family without even saying goodbye. "Have you seen Hassan, Bibi?" I asked. "Oh yes, child. He's at the cinema today. Come, let's make tea." Bibi would respond with something new every day.

I never knew where he went. I always had to ask his family where he was. He would go shopping and to parks and cinemas all alone. It would've been nice if he'd take me with him. But I never asked him to take me with him because I was afraid he would beat me and ignore me again. Bibi tried her best to make me feel comfortable at home, but nothing ever made me feel okay again.

When that summer was about to end and schools were starting again, Bibi called me over to talk. "Okay, honey. It's time to go to Bushehr. So I want you to pack up, okay? All your *j*aaris are ready to go. We're going to leave next week, so that should give you enough time." Bushehr is a small but important port in southern Iran along the coastline of the Persian Gulf. I was very confused. "Why? Is it a vacation?" I asked. "A vacation?" Bibi was shocked that I even asked that. "*This* is our vacation home." She looked at me, concerned. "Bushehr is where we *actually* live. Of course, it is also your new home now," she added. "But…Shiraz is my home," I said quietly. "Oh, don't be afraid. Bushehr is beautiful, you'll love it there." Her words shocked me. I had no idea that they lived in Bushehr. I had no idea that I would have to live so far away from my family. My mother and father never told me this when they were telling me about Hassan. How could they possibly do this to me? Why did my parents choose Hassan? Now I would never actually see my family. No. It's impossible, I thought. My parents would not let them take me away from them. I wanted to run home and scream at my parents, "Help me! Rescue me! Take me back please! He is not a Prince Charming; he is the villain of my fairy tale!" I remembered a story that my mother used to tell us. It was about a giant, ugly monster that kidnapped a little girl, making her his prisoner forever. She had to wash the monster's clothes, clean his house, and cook for him. I realized that I was that little girl. I remember being so scared when she told us this story. Alas! I never knew that it would become my life one day.

I had the chance to see my family before we left. As soon as I saw my mother I confronted her. "Why didn't you tell me that I would be forced to move? You never once told me that he lived in Bushehr!" I had never spoken to my mother this way before.

"What are you ranting about? You are not going to live there! They had told me they were just going to take you there once a year," my mother said defensively. I couldn't find it in myself to believe her. She knew I would go to Bushehr.

"What did once a year mean to you?" I couldn't hold back this time. "They meant once a year they go back home for nine months and then come back every summer!" I was angry. "How could you do this to me? I don't know them. I want my family back. I want to come back home, go to school," I yelled. My mother had a smirk on her face.

"That's your destiny. I cannot change your destiny. You were probably meant to live in Bushehr. Stop complaining and go live your life. You are not supposed to live with your parents forever. Do not behave like a child. You are a married woman. Deal with your problems. Can't you see I have enough problems?" She lit a cigarette and began to smoke. "Everybody has to deal with their own problems. I don't like my daughters to come home and talk about their problems. I have enough of my own." And just like that, she was finished with the conversation. No longer interested. Maybe she told Amene the same things when she came home to us. My mother never liked people who had problems. She used to say, "They make me sad." She never visited sad relatives nor invited them over because she did not like to feel sad. I was sure she would not think about me, because it would make her sad.

I told Bibi about how no one told me that I was supposed to move to Bushehr. Bibi said that she had informed my mother that if Hassan married me, I was to move to Bushehr with them at the end of the summer of my wedding. But my mother even denied ever hearing that. I felt like she knew. I could never be absolutely sure if my mother was telling the truth or not. But I had already gotten the impression that Bibi was a much more kind and honest woman than my mother. And I was almost always certain that a woman like Bibi would not leave out telling my mother and father that they were going to take me to Bushehr. My parents not only took away my youth, but they also took away everything that I had of my childhood to remember: the place that I grew up in. At least if I lived in Shiraz, I would walk down the same streets that Masume and I did when we walked to school. Or I'd visit the same candy store that Amene and I would shop at all the time, just to get a reminder of the times that I was still a kid. Those streets I walked and the stores I went to were not in Bushehr. It was like destroying my memory lane. I would not be able to go home to visit my family. These thoughts made me cry a lot, but I tried not to show it. If Hassan ever saw me crying, he'd beat me. I figured, even if I told my mother that Hassan was physically abusive, she would just yell and say, "Do not be a child. Go home and solve your own problems." I decided to follow the rules and obey, hoping that if at least my husband stopped hitting me, then maybe my other problems would be solved easily. I was going to miss everything I had, and moving away felt like letting go of my whole life. I was going to miss my father and mother even though they would not miss me. I was going to miss my brothers and sisters. I was going to miss everyone and everything.

Regardless of whom the liar was, my parents or Bibi, I had to move without a choice. I packed all my belongings and set my little suitcase aside. I looked for my small bucket where I had kept all the gold coins that I got as wedding gifts. That bucket contained at least two kilograms, if not more, of gold coins, which was a lot of money. I could probably buy a house with that much gold back in those days. I searched for it everywhere, but could not find it. I asked Hassan's family if they had seen my bucket of gold coins. "There are a lot of mice in this house. Maybe they stole your coins." Hassan's brother laughed. I was eleven, but I wasn't stupid. Mice could not carry a single coin; how could they possibly be able to carry a bucket? I was sure they took my gold coins, but I couldn't do anything about it because Hassan was involved for sure and they all knew about it. He could hit me again, so I just shut my mouth like always. I sat beside my suitcase and cried, for as long as a clock could keep track of. I was unable to tell myself that it was going to be okay.

Hassan came and took my suitcase to put it in the trunk of his car. Two of Hassan's brothers sat in the front seats of Hassan's Opel. Hassan drove while Bibi, my sisters-in-law, their kids, and I all sat in the back. There was no law at that time to restrict the number of passengers in a car and it was not unusual for one single car to carry that many people. Not many people had cars, so they were filled with as many passengers as possible. I looked out of the window and decided that I was going to accept my new beginning.

Nowadays, a drive to Bushehr is only four to five hours long from Shiraz, but back then the drive took more than twelve hours. The reason was because there were only dirt roads and we had to drive along steep mountains with narrow roads, which required a slow and cautious drive. Some of the roads were so narrow along the mountains that two cars could not fit in side by side. So you had to wait by the very edge of the mountain for a car to pass by. It was a very scary trip, since the car could fall off the edge of the mountain at any moment. Buses and big trucks were the most common vehicles on the roads with dark, thick, black smoke coming out of their exhausts, making it hard for the passengers in the small cars behind them to see or breathe. You could see many buses or trucks, which were just parked on the roadside, waiting for their engine to cool down because it was a long drive.

The drive to Bushehr was very dangerous and frustrating apart from being extremely long. Hassan drove all the way, even though he was the youngest brother, but he was the only one who had a driver's license. At one point during the road trip, our car broke down and we were stuck in the middle of nowhere. Hassan didn't look frustrated at all, which he never did when he was around his own family. "I'll take a look at it and see what the problem is," he said. He even joked about it constantly to lighten everyone's mood. He got out of the car and popped up the trunk. I watched him as he studied the engine, doing a few magical things. Within around an hour the problem was fixed, and the car was working again. Hassan's passion for cars was not a lie, I thought. He was actually becoming a mechanical engineer. While he was fixing the car, his family spread out a carpet outside for everyone to sit on. They even prepared tea and enjoyed that hour of waiting, as if they were on a picnic. If my family had been in this situation, my father would have sworn at my mother and she would have sworn back using harsher words.

Along the way of our trip, we had two or three picnics to eat, rest, and make the commute less difficult and more enjoyable. They seriously loved it, and I was learning from them that you should enjoy even the hardest moments of life. And I learned that Hassan was more calm and happy with his family and that he loved driving. I learned to accept my situation, and be like them and laugh at and enjoy everything. We finally got there, where I was stepping into my new life. I tried to be positive and started to smile at my destiny.

—⁂—

Chapter 8

Hassan's father's generosity and honesty led to the growth of his merchandising business over the years. He used to travel to India and take Bibi with him. The trips took months, and she could not be away from him for such a long time because she loved him very much. In India, he used to buy merchandise that was considered good for Iran and ship it to Bushehr, and they always traveled back to Iran on that ship. Bushehr was one of the three important ports in the south of Iran, which was also closest to Shiraz.

One year when they arrived back at the port with their merchandise, Hassan's father found out that the roads between Bushehr and Shiraz were completely flooded, making it impossible to travel through the roads for months. As they were the kind of family that enjoyed life even in the worst of circumstances, and he was also very rich, he bought the best chain stores in downtown Bushehr along with the biggest mansion made by British architects hundreds of years back. I was told that it was built by the English engineers to stay in while they were in Iran for oil discovery. He filled up his stores with the merchandise that he had brought from India, and waited for the flood to recede and the roads to Shiraz to reopen. They were living without any communication with Shiraz for almost a year. But they were beginning to really enjoy living in Bushehr. They loved the mansion and the business was going very well too. Hassan's father became very well-known in town because of how honest, polite, smart, and generous he was. Even after the floods, they continued to live in Bushehr and went back to their big house in Shiraz during the summers to distribute their imported merchandise in Shiraz.

As we drove through Bushehr, I could see the difference between Bushehr and Shiraz. Bushehr seemed more like a very small village than a city. Everything looked very different. The majority of the houses were mud huts, which were the size of a single room. It seemed like people were very poor there. You could see the piles of garbage everywhere as if there was no one from the city to pick it up. There was only one street for commuting and it was always covered in a thick layer of dirt. Car tires sank in almost halfway through the dirt and created a thick cloud of dust as they drove along. Whenever there was rain, the dirt road turned into a big muddy mess, so much so that the cars couldn't even pass through.

"We're almost home!" Bibi smiled and looked at me. We turned into a street with Hassan's last name. "It's because of all the good things my husband did for this town," Bibi said as she saw me reading the sign. I did not see houses lined up next to one another; I just saw one gigantic property spanning from the beginning to the end of the street, surrounded by high walls. Hassan pressed the horn a few times until a middle-aged man opened a big blue wooden door with a huge iron arch design on the top, which was the entrance through the high walls that bordered the property. "Welcome back!" The man waved as Hassan drove in. He was the caretaker, who had been living in two rooms near the iron door with his wife and three children. His duty was to open the door for them, walk around the property and make sure there was no garbage around and clear the dead leaves and branches, garden, and mostly guard the place especially when they were away in Shiraz.

Past the high walls lay a mansion that equally spanned the street from one end to the other. Hassan parked his car and began unloading everything while Bibi welcomed me to my new home. I stood there stealing glimpses of the mansion. I had never seen anything like it. And I instantly fell in love with it. Its British architecture made it stand out from all the other buildings that I had ever seen before. It stood there, an intricate stack of bricks, mud, and cement, stretching high into the sky, a heaven in the middle of hell. It was 150 years old, becoming imprinted with memories and antiquity with each passing year, something that only comes with time. Every side of the house had a set of stairs that led to an entrance. Each entrance led to a separate unit for each of the three brothers and Bibi to live.

In the very beginning, only Bibi and her husband lived in this huge mansion. Bibi gave birth to a son every four years. She used to say she never planned to have kids every four years and God gave them to her in this order. When their father passed away, the sons became the owners of the stores and the mansion and took over the business. Every brother had three huge rooms, and they had prepared three rooms for Hassan and me as well. Bibi had her own room. Hassan was the youngest brother. His second brother lived in Shiraz in the big house, where I had gotten married, which was also a summer house for all the brothers. He had four daughters, and his oldest daughter was a year younger than me. Hassan's oldest brother was eighteen years older than him, and had three daughters and one son. They lived in the rooms on the east side of the house. His daughter was about my age, but she had not been married off. His third brother and his wife lived in the rooms on the northeast side of the house with their two sons. His fourth brother had one daughter and one son, and he had rooms that faced the Persian Gulf. There were still two huge rooms left in the house that were used just for special occasions, and were always ready and clean for accommodating the formal guests.

Every room was connected to beautiful open hallways with antique wooden fences. You could see the sea out in the distance from one of the building's sides when you stood by the fence. I had never seen the sea before. It was beautiful. I was completely mesmerized. The rooms were so huge that anybody could freely and easily run around in them. Each room had very high ceilings that were covered with logs of wood and had eight gorgeous narrow antique wooden doors, which each had six small panes of glass on it and an arched stained glass window at the top. The mansion was designed to circulate air and make the rooms cooler as Bushehr's weather was mild during the winters and hot during the summers.

Each part of the house had a kitchen, but there were no bathrooms upstairs, as all those facilities were downstairs along with the huge storage spaces, where they kept all the merchandise. There were beautiful vintage drawers and armoires that were left behind by their English owners.

There was a big lime garden to the east of the house that had approximately one hundred lime trees. In the southeast of the house lay a beautiful pond with a cement gazebo over it. There was a small brown wooden door that opened to the other street around the house, but no one ever used that door. On the north side, there was a very big open storage area, and in the south of the house there was a long pathway surrounded by beautiful trees and flowers that led to the main door, where we had entered from. Each side of the huge property had a door that opened to another street or alley.

The home was very inviting. I felt secure and I knew I wouldn't get tired of this place.

Chapter 9

Living in Bushehr felt like I was living a few decades back in time than the time I was born into. Everything was unusual because the city wasn't developed. It was very out-of-date; there were no pipelines for water and we had to get water from the ponds and wells, which were not filtered at all, and not safe to drink for sure. Many people in Bushehr had diseases because of the polluted water. Their skin would puff up and worms would live and multiply beneath it. They had to make slits on their skin to make openings for the worms to get out, which miraculously did not kill them. The majority of the people in Bushehr had lice. Hygiene and health were not very popular things to encounter there. It was heartbreaking to look at so many people with diseases. We did not have the dirty water issue because we boiled our water to get rid of the bacteria that led to illnesses. We always washed our hair to make sure we did not get lice. But in reality, the border between Shiraz and Bushehr was like stepping into a time machine. You could never see any asphalt on the streets. There was only one small bazaar and one hospital, which looked more like a walk-in clinic.

Every morning Hassan went to an industrial high school where he taught and worked very hard and seriously. After school he came back home at 3:00 p.m. and ate a quick lunch and went back to his father's shop with his brothers and worked there until 9:00 p.m., which was its closing time. His brothers worked since morning and came home for lunch too. Their schedule was always like this. Their main merchants were those who dealt in home appliances—big and small— and hardware. I did not mind Hassan's working all those hours; the more he was out of the house, the more fun I could have. Every Friday, which was everyone's day off, we used to cook a big pot of Persian food for lunch and prepare something for dinner as well, and pack everything up and put it into Hassan's car. All the family members, that is, nine adults and eight kids, would fit into the car. How did we possibly fit into one car? There must have been more love and closeness and kindness then. You cannot find such closeness these days. We all piled up on one another's laps and kept laughing until we got to the destination, which was always a long distance. Hassan's family did not mind driving a long way as long as the view was nice. We had lots of fun with all the eating and laughing and playing different games with balls or the traditional games. Bushehr's weather in fall and winter and spring was delightful, and most of the time even in the winter you could go on a picnic. We used to go to the beach Heleyleh very often. We all loved sitting by the sea and staring into the distance and walking on the sandy shore. The view of the sea for me, who'd never lived by the sea, was spectacular. Life with them was much more fun only if Hassan acted like a different person. But, no matter how great the sea looked and how fun being with the family was, I missed Shiraz and being with my family. I missed my grumpy father and my careless mother and my sisters and brothers, especially my little nephew, Mohammad, and everyone there. I missed breathing Shiraz's air and the smell of its blossoms and the crowd and the asphalt.

Bibi was a moral soul. You would think that every mother-in-law is harsh and inequitable, but Bibi did not act like my mother-in-law; she acted like the mother I never had. During the initial days of my marriage, I did not know much about cooking and cleaning. How could I? My mother did not give us a chance to learn these skills from her, not that she really knew much anyway. To Hassan, I was not much of a good housewife. His expectations of an eleven-year-old child were selfish and unfair. Bibi understood that expecting an eleven-year-old to have the knowledge of a housewife was absurd; this is why I said Bibi was an intelligent woman. Bibi on the other hand, seemed like she knew exactly what an eleven-year-old would think, and that was why I felt like she was the only one in that small, crazy world who understood me. It made me trust her and get close to her more and more every day and even love her more.

Getting married makes you realize many things; one thing I realized from my marriage was how different our lifestyles were. I never really showed it, but I felt like Hassan's family lived in a much better way than mine. My mother had interest in many things, but never in cooking and cleaning, among other chores. Bibi was the exact opposite of my mother. Bibi loved cooking; she was a very clean woman. But most of all she had talents in things, like knitting and sewing along with other different crafts. Because of her generous and kind personality she shared her skills with me. I never told Bibi, no matter how much I trusted her, that I had never seen half the things she taught me in my own home. I never put my family down and never talked about them unless it was something good or mostly lies; there really were not many positive things to talk about, except for my father's fame and my parents' fortune and that would be showing off, as my sisters-in-law came from poor families. When Bibi taught me how to cook traditional Persian meals, I acted like I had seen my mother do it all before. She showed me spices like saffron, the most luxurious spice in the world, which my mom never used. She told me secrets about her ways of cooking and baking, which I applied every time I cooked for the rest of my life. She was a very good cook and she made me a great cook. And because my mother never put any effort into teaching us anything or even spending time with us, I liked Bibi and how she took time for me and was patient and kind during her teaching. She never yelled at me and made me uncomfortable, and even if I made any little mistakes she just smiled and said everyone makes mistakes, and not to worry because we learn from our mistakes. I felt happy and loved and free with her. The more time I spent with Bibi, the closer we became. I wished all my twenty-four hours of the day could be during the daytime, so I could be safe and happy beside Bibi and learn so much.

Everyone who lived in the house had separate kitchens, but most days they all would gather in the main kitchen and cook together; they helped one another and talked and told stories or jokes and laughed. Their way of living enabled them to enjoy their lifestyle without complaining and not get bored. If only Hassan would have stopped hitting me, then maybe I could have adjusted to their lifestyle. In the afternoon, the ladies used to sit together in different parts of the house with great views and mostly great weather, and spread a carpet and have tea, cakes, and cookies. Every single day was like a picnic, and all the ladies would do different kinds of art; some knitted, some sewed and some embroidered. Bibi taught me these skills and I learned better than others. I realized how much I loved handicrafts. When it was dinnertime and the men came back home, all the members of the family would gather together. They would assemble their meals like a potluck of the food that we had cooked together, would spread a big cloth on the floor in one of the brothers' living rooms every time and sit around it to eat. We would all try one another's foods, and have fun, like each Friday of the summers when we used to go to my father's garden. Only this fun was an everyday routine. I loved eating with them. After dinner we all sat together and had tea and fruits and talked. Their days were always like this. Every Saturday, which was the first day of the week, was the laundry day. Nobody had washing machines back in those days. People had to wash their clothes by hand. We all gathered by the pond and washed our clothes and hung all of them and had lots of fun. And I wished every day we would wash clothes and sheets. I washed Bibi's clothes, not that she asked me to, but I insisted; we did not have as many clothes as the others because I had no child.

We all washed the dishes the morning after each night. They piled all the dishes in the pond room that was made for washing the dishes during the winters because of the cold weather. After breakfast, which everybody had separately, and after the men left for work, we all would gather in the pond room and enjoy washing hundreds of dishes all at once that were piled up from the previous night. I could wash the dishes like this forever and never get tired because they all made it look like lots of fun. And Bibi was always with us, just sitting on a chair somewhere close; no one would let her do anything as she was an old woman. She was like a kind supervisor.

I got more attached to Bibi and did everything for her. I was pleased to take care of her, like taking care of a kind old grandmother. I walked slowly with her, talked to her a lot, and listened to her stories. I loved her stories, asked all the questions that a little girl has in mind, and she loved to answer. I asked her how she felt every day and if she took her medicines, and made sure she ate anything I knew was good for her. Sometimes I put my head on her lap and close my eyes and thought, which I never did with my mother. My mother never let us get close to her: she never felt like answering nonsense questions. I easily asked the stupidest questions to Bibi and she would giggle and laugh, but she never pushed me away. She was with me every minute. I needed someone in my life like Bibi and because she did not have any daughters, she loved all the attention. I was not Bibi's only daughter-in-law, but I could certainly say I was her favorite. There were so many times when she whispered that I was the daughter she never had. My sisters-in-law were older than me by several years. Some were more or less my mother's age, while I was the same age as their kids. They did not really like me at first because I was from a rich and well-known family. But that never bothered me. Even though I was a child, I was a smart and positive person and always liked them. I had no one in Bushehr, and I for sure wanted to have friends and not enemies. No matter how they felt, I got closer and closer to them. It made me more confident about myself. Although it took a while, soon they realized that I was a friendly person. They started approaching me slowly and with each passing day, we became closer. I gained their trust, and eventually they shared their secrets with me that they knew I would keep to myself. We were all prisoners of a heavenly castle; I needed them and we all needed one another.

I respected a lot of the differences that my family had from Hassan's because a lot of the alterations that I saw were good changes. I experienced the atmosphere of having a loving mother, who cooked and cleaned and cared and loved her children, courtesy of Bibi. Not that I suddenly forgot about my own mother and replaced the memories of her with Bibi. But there were a lot of things my mother lacked that Bibi had. Having said that, there is one thing my mother conquered that Bibi needed: style. Bibi would order the finest fabrics from foreign countries that were very expensive. However, the problem was that she gave the fabrics to the tailor, who would sew dozens of the same garments out of them. This led to the biggest setback: all the children and women of the house wore the same thing. My mother always dressed us based on what was "in vogue" in Europe. Bibi and the rest of her family seemed unaware of the fashion world. I missed the way my mother used to dress me and my sisters and did not like wearing the same thing as everybody else. I did wear them at first, but I had to learn to stand up to the things I did not like or else they would change me completely, and I liked to be me.

As time passed, I began to get a better glimpse of reality. I was hit with the cold, hard truth. I was forced to marry an abusive man. And I found myself sugarcoating it all. Maybe this was ordinary. Maybe this was *okay*. I wanted really badly for Hassan to love me, to protect me. I wanted him to touch me gently. But time showed me the truth. Hassan hurt me intentionally, for foolish reasons. No matter how careful I was about my actions, in Hassan's eyes, I still made mistakes. I tried my best not to even move when he came back from work, but I guess he took anything that bothered him in the world out on me and hit me, kicked me, punched me, and slapped me. His hands were so heavy that the pressure he put into his hand while hitting was crushing. He had a spark in his eyes that ignited a wildfire and that sent him into a rage. Bruises and pain became ordinary. Black-and-blue colors stained my skin, as if they had always been a part of me. I couldn't imagine waking up one day with unharmed flesh. There wasn't a night that I didn't cry myself to sleep. But I never screamed or cried out loud. I had pride. I barely slept at night. I stayed up, focusing on distancing my body from his and hating what my parents had done to me and wondering why I was there. Thank you, Mother and Father! Good night and I love you, I said to myself every single night. I wondered who he hit before he married me. Or maybe he saved all his power for his wife. I guess he should have married a punching bag instead. It was very important for me to show others that we were doing well; I wanted to fit in with his family. Pretending like we were happy was the only happiness I could feel. Hassan's brothers were very kind to their wives. I had never even seen them disrespect or hit their wives. No one in the household had bruises except me. I couldn't imagine that Hassan's brothers hit their wives in their rooms secretly, like Hassan hit me. Their marriages were genuine and happy. They were kind to their wives and their wives were kind to them. But Hassan always disrespected me with words and made fun of me and my family in front of his family. They all laughed, and I had to smile or else he would hit me later in our room. I was sure Bibi knew he hit me. I was sure all the brothers knew it too because of the way I walked in pain and the bruises, but no one ever said a word. Every morning, when new marks were added on my skin, Bibi would just look at me in a sad way. But she'd never mention them to me. It was something we all just didn't talk about. No matter how close we got, I never complained about Hassan to Bibi. Even though he was her son, Bibi always stood up for me in my absence, behind closed doors. I would hide and listen to her scolding Hassan. Once I remember, I was sewing in the yard with my sisters-in-law. I went back inside to make tea, and that's when I heard Bibi crying from afar. I had traced her voice and found her in her room with Hassan. I had hidden in the corridor where they couldn't see me, but I could hear them. "Please, Hassan! Please. Leave the girl alone! She's only a child!" Bibi cried in between her words. I watched tears rolling down her cheeks, tears that were being shed for me. I had felt loved and cared about, something I'd never really felt from my own mother. The only embrace I felt from my mother was through the gift boxes she sent to me. She would sew clothes and shoes and would pay the bus drivers to bring them to Bushehr. I really enjoyed being pampered and felt a bit spoiled too. I loved the attention, as it made me feel like they had not forgotten me. Maybe somewhere deep down she felt sorry for me, and reckoned it was her fault that I was living life this way. My mother was a very complicated woman and if I were to live a day having her mind, I think I would go insane trying to figure her out, but I was glad that she did send me gifts. Bibi showed her love through words and food. Maybe the only way my mother knew how to express her affection was through fashion. I needed to be loved. I was only a kid and was happy that she had not forgotten that. "As your mother, every time you lay your hands on that child, it feels like you're hitting me. You're using your fists to destroy me, as you torment her!" Hassan just stood there, watching her speak. He focused on her words, but he didn't respond. "I will stop praying for you, Hassan. Hurting an innocent child is a sin. It's forbidden! What would your father have said?!" At the mention of his father, Hassan's expression changed, and his eyes became glossy. "Get closer to God. Change this disgusting habit. The way you are going is not God's path." As I heard Bibi scold Hassan, I felt the pain in my chest lessen, but the pain in my flesh and bones remained. Her love was strong, and it cradled me. I was grateful for her. But as much as Hassan loved and respected his mother, he didn't stop hitting me. It was something uncontrollable for him, and seemed like a part of his identity, like a fingerprint. The way I wanted to dress differently from other members of his family made Hassan angrier, and he hit me again and again. But I did not care and wore what pleased me. I felt victorious when finally; Hassan stopped hitting me for what I wore. Well, he always had other reasons. But it was a revolution in the house, and they all learned that they were free to choose their own clothes and they did. We used to look ridiculous, but then we all looked better. I was only a child, but I knew I could not make Hassan stop hitting me, because I had a small, weak body and lacked the power to hit him back, but I had the power to stand up for myself in different ways, and I would not let him abuse me in any other part of my life. I always knew that in any fight one of the contenders would get tired and give up. Between Hassan and me, I knew that person would not be me. Let him hit me as much as he wanted; I did not care. He would get bored and tired one day. I could not wait for that day, or maybe it was not really important to me any longer.

Chapter 10

LIFE FOR ME BECAME A ROUTINE. I WOKE UP WITH LESS and less passion as the days passed by. I cried every day after Hassan left for work, and put on a good dress and my mask of happiness and made the best of each day. I felt like I was living a life scripted by the people around me. Children get excited about little things and somewhere I still had that inside of me. Bibi showed me a lot of things that stunned me and motivated me, but Hassan did a lot of things that crushed me and stole my hope. The little energy and joy that pushed me to be able to follow routine and be quiet about my sorrows was the group I lived with, ignoring my sadness and weakness. I lived like a rag doll that was thrown anywhere and would just land somewhere powerlessly.

Finally, nine months of long, hard nights and days passed, and it was time to travel back to Shiraz for three summer months.

Hassan did not work during the three summer months, so we all went to stay in their home in Shiraz. They never closed the store back in Bushehr, so one brother would stay for a month, then the other one would come and replace him, and then the third brother, but Hassan never went back to Bushehr in the summer. I wish he would have, so I could have spent one month alone with my family. All my jaaris would be in Shiraz for three whole months, since Bushehr's weather was very hot, and almost impossible to bear for us, but for people born in Bushehr, the scorching summer sun was normal.

Packing and driving back to Shiraz on the long, dangerous, muddy road was exciting this time, because I would be able to see my city and most of all my family again. I had never been away from them for a single day before. Finally, after twelve hours of driving we were in Shiraz by night. As we drove through the city, I couldn't stop smiling. The streetlights and pine trees made me feel nostalgic. I felt like I was home. I wished that we could drive directly to my parent's house. I wanted to be in a place where I could cry loudly, breaking the silence that I had forced upon myself for nine months. As we drove through the city, I daydreamed about my mother holding me in her arms and looking into my eyes while she combed my hair with her fingers. She would say, "You're home now, Najma. You're safe. You're never leaving again. I'll keep you safe, baby. I promise and won't let them take you to Bushehr again." I snapped back into reality as we arrived at their home. As I walked through the house, moments from my wedding night kept playing in my mind. I could see people laughing and crowding up the corridors, waiters and waitresses serving food and drinks, and live music playing in the background. Then I saw my mother, laughing and telling stories to her friends, having the time of her life. In that moment, the crowd disappeared. The food was gone. The music stopped playing, and it was just my mother and me face-to-face. "What are you doing standing there? Get back to your husband. You have duties as a wife." My mother's eyes were empty and frightening. "Please help me. Please," I cried. "You're an adult now, a married woman. You have to fix your own problems." She laughed as she walked away.

Bibi and all my brothers-in-law and their wives, including Hassan and me, got a room to ourselves in the house.

The distance between my family and I was hardly there when we stayed in Shiraz, but somehow, I couldn't say the same about emotional distance. Hassan always tried to separate me from them. I wanted to visit them a lot since I was in the same city as them, but Hassan had limited me to seeing them for a maximum of once a week, from 10:00 a.m. to 4:00

p.m. And he would not come there more than once a month, which was fine by me. I had been away from my family long enough. I deserved to be with them every second. But instead, I had to be with his family again and do all the routine things we did for the whole nine months in our summer as well. Not that I did not appreciate their company, but I just wanted to be with my family.

There were so many moments when I had the urge to just look Hassan right in the eyes and scream, "What is your problem! Let me live! Let me breathe! Leave me alone!" but I couldn't. All I knew was that Hassan had a problem. He was a foolish man and I could not change it. He threatened to hurt me if I came home a minute later than 4:00 p.m. after visiting my family. I hated knowing that his words were true. Hassan was not afraid to hurt me; nothing ashamed him about raising his hands and thrashing his own wife in rage. Nothing ashamed him about hurting a child. Although physically I was with my family, my soul spanned through daunting thoughts of the things Hassan would do to me if I returned late. All the times that I was with my family, I concentrated on being careful not to go home later than 4:00 p.m. He knew that this way I would not enjoy my time with them, and he knew it would ruin my day. That was all that he wanted. He enjoyed hurting me. But what I did not understand was why.

All the times when I went back home one of my close relatives would organize a big lunch and gather all the family, so I could see them all. Of course, Hassan never attended. They always asked me why my husband never accompanied me, and I had to lie, again and again. I hated how I always let Hassan get to me, no matter how hard I tried to be as self-regulating as I could be. The person you love is supposed to be on your mind all day, making you happy just by thinking about them. Hassan did make me think about him every second from 10:00 a.m. to 4:00 p.m., but those were never any good thoughts, just always fear of the clock showing 3:30

p.m. The very thought of him frightened me.

One time when I was with my family I had more fun than usual with all my cousins, and Hassan still crossed my mind, but I was more neutral than I was on the other days that I had visited. When I looked at the clock, I realized I was late. My heart raced, and my eyes started to water. I hoped that Hassan would let it go, but sometimes hope lets you down the most. I only got home fifteen minutes late. Fifteen minutes. I walked in and unsurprisingly Hassan had been waiting for me. His eyes were filled with fury, and mine with tears. He was standing next to my favorite high heels, which were broken, and my favorite dress was torn apart. He cursed at me, humiliated me in front of everyone. "Look at the time!" he screamed. I stayed silent. "Look at the time!" he yelled even louder. I cried loudly for once. Right in front him, right in front of everyone. His family was telling him to stop. Telling him to leave me alone, speaking the words that I wanted to say. He dragged me to our room and hit me so hard that I would never be late again, for the rest of my life. He kept hitting me, one punch after the other, aiming for my head. This time not only my body hurt, but also my soul, my feelings, and my pride were crushed and shattered. I felt the worst feeling a human could ever feel. I never wanted to look into his family's eyes again. I was ashamed. I wanted to die. I wanted to hit him, slap him so hard that he'd never lay his hands on me again, but I couldn't. I stayed silent as he hit me, taunting me about my broken heels and my ripped dress. He wouldn't stop hitting me. He had never gone this far before. This time he was not stopping. His brothers jumped into our room and tried to hold him back. "Stop it. Stop it, Hassan! You'll kill her!" they yelled. Bibi was crying and screaming at him. "Look at what you're doing to this beautiful child. Look at what you're doing! How could you do this! How could you?!" She was trying to hold me, to come in between his blows.

When I woke up the next morning, Hassan acted like nothing had happened. I felt like Hassan had glitches in his system; he went crazy, and then suddenly he was back to normal. No one outside of Hassan's family knew that he had a habit of hurting me. They all fantasized that Hassan and I had a happy marriage, all thanks to me. I could have told the whole world about how much of a bad husband Hassan was, but I chose not to. From an outsider's perspective, it would've been hard to believe that he was abusive. Hassan portrayed himself as a funny, extremely polite, well-spoken, well-mannered, educated, neat, and good-looking gentleman, whom everybody respected and loved. The way that he carried himself was very deceiving. I was disgusted when I watched him at gatherings. Many girls probably wished that they were his wife. If only they knew the real man that he was when he was alone with me.

I never liked anybody to pity me. Telling people how Hassan was acting would not have gotten me protection from him. It would just upset people, and they would move on with their lives while I lingered in the same spot as I was at before.

My mother felt sorry for me, only because I had to live in Bushehr. I never told her that he hit me because I was sure she wouldn't care, neither would my father. They would say be patient, and that time would eventually solve all the problems. So what was the point? I just didn't have a shoulder to cry on.

Chapter 11

Summer ended and we had to go back to Bushehr. I just rode along with life, as I was supposed to. I was grateful for the little time I got to spend with my family. I knew that Hassan had the power to forbid me from ever seeing them again, so I was thankful that he even allowed those short hours, and I looked forward to the next summer when I would get the chance to see them again.

I was thirteen the first time I got my period. I had no idea what had happened to me. I was terrified. I thought it was because I was raped time and again and my body suddenly couldn't take it anymore. I knew if I told Hassan, he would hit me and blame me for doing something wrong and letting this happen to me. But I couldn't just keep it to myself. I had to make up my mind and tell someone because I didn't know what to do about the blood. I didn't know what was wrong with me. I was embarrassed to tell anybody else in the home, so I decided to just risk it and tell Hassan. Surprisingly, Hassan didn't hit me. He didn't even raise his voice. In fact, he smiled. "You're going to be okay," he reassured me. "This is natural, this is good for us." He told me that I was a woman now. But I was a woman long before my period; my body had just caught up.

During my period, Hassan was kinder to me. In fact, he was proud of me, as if I had accomplished something. At night, he would say good night and lie next to me without forcing himself onto me, without raping me. But this ended as soon as my period did. I learned to track my periods. I understood that they came once a month. I was told to expect it. The next month, I got my period around the same time.

But the month after, a week passed by my expected time and I didn't see any blood. I was so afraid. I didn't know if something was wrong with me. Hassan was very nice to me when I got my period; I wondered if he would get angry when he found out that I had missed it this month. This time I knew that all women got their periods, so I was less shy to talk about it. I didn't want to risk telling Hassan anything, so I went to Bibi instead. "Oh, honey! Poor child must be so frightened. Don't be afraid, dear. This is exciting!" Bibi put her arm around my shoulders. "You're going to be a mother! You have a baby growing inside of you!" My eyes opened wide. I didn't know how to feel at that time. All I could think about was the times that I played house with Amene and Masume. It was all about playing pretend then; I didn't know how to be a mother. I was still learning how to hide being a child and pretend to be an adult. I didn't feel ready. Yet another part of me was excited. I wanted to hold a baby in my arms that I could call my own. Amene had Mohammad and she had managed just fine. On top of that, I had Bibi and I knew she would teach me everything she knew and help me in every way that she could. This made me feel better.

Hassan was really happy about my pregnancy. I had never seen him so excited about something that involved me before. For once I had made him happy. I felt accomplished. It was very important for him to become a father. I could see it in his eyes that he had been waiting for this moment for a long time. I saw a gentleness that I had seen in Hassan on the night of our wedding when he had held my hand. I thought maybe he had changed. Maybe this was what he had wanted from me all this time, and now that I finally gave it to him, he'd be kinder to me and stop hitting me. I thought maybe this was the turning point in our relationship. Our whole lives were about to change for the better. I cared about Hassan, but he never acknowledged it, which never gave me a chance to grow my feelings for him. If he could just let our love unmask, we could be happy. I felt, at times, that he truly loved me, but he just didn't show it. I wanted to hold on to that. I wanted him to embrace our duality, the way his brothers embraced their wives. But Hassan's happiness proved to be temporary. It was that very night when he slammed me into the wall and beat my face until he felt like stopping. He continued to hit me throughout my pregnancy, making sure to aim for my head to keep the baby safe. After he'd hit me, he'd torture me with silence for weeks to come, sometimes for as long as a month. Then whenever he pleased he would ask me to beg him to talk to me again. "Kiss my hand if you want us to talk again," he'd say. "Now kiss my feet." He'd laugh. And I'd do it. I'd get down on my knees with my baby in my stomach, and I'd kiss his feet.

One of my jaaris was pregnant with her fifth, another one with her fourth, and two of them with their third child when I was pregnant. Bibi really took care of me, in particular. She fed me everything and anything that I desired. She loved me and pampered me. I was very fortunate to have her. One day when Bibi and I were alone baking together she said, "You're like a daughter to me. All I've got are sons. And I love them, God bless them. But I always wanted a daughter, and God sent me you."

I remember tears instantly flooded my eyes. "You're like a mother to me, Bibi," I responded.

"I mean it, Najma. I've four other daughters-in-law, but I don't consider you as one. You really are precious to me. You're the daughter I never had. I want you to remember that always. And I did. I felt her nurturing and warm embrace from the moment that I met her. She was like a mother to me, a mother I never had.

As months passed, I noticed my stomach getting very abnormally large to a point where I couldn't move a lot. I had seen many pregnant women, and I'd never seen their stomachs as big as mine. When I reached the eighth month in my pregnancy, Hassan took me to Shiraz. Since we were from Shiraz, it was Hassan's family tradition to bring their pregnant wives back, so their children could be born in their home city. I was surprised that Hassan even allowed it. I just hoped that he'd let me see my family a lot more often. I felt so debilitated with my large stomach and I needed them. But he didn't. He took me to his house in Shiraz and forbade me from visiting my family unless he allowed it, which was very rare.

After my brother Ebrahim was born, my mother had difficulty getting pregnant. She spent a lot of money and time at the doctor's trying to get pregnant again. When Hassan brought me to Shiraz, I found out that my mother was pregnant again after trying for nine years. She had kept it a secret. I thought about my mother and me having a child of the same age. It was very uncomfortable for me. I didn't understand why she wanted it so badly, to have more children. She already had sons-in-law and grandchildren. And she was about to have a child younger than her own grandson and granddaughter, as Amene had given birth to a beautiful baby girl too. I was embarrassed by my mother's pregnancy. I couldn't understand it, and neither could anybody else in Shiraz. But my mother wasn't embarrassed or ashamed of course. In fact, she was proud of herself. Having babies was like a competition for her. It made her feel young. She always talked about how doctors told her to fight her depression by getting pregnant and having children. I doubt that was any doctor's suggestion for a grandmother. It was a self-prescribed rejuvenation for her. During the rare moments when Hassan allowed me to visit my parents, my mother was always too busy dealing with her own pregnancy to acknowledge that I was even there.

After being in Shiraz for a few weeks, extremely painful contractions erupted, and I knew that it was finally the time for delivery. Hassan was getting everything ready. I was prepared to get in the car to go to the hospital when Hassan's brother stopped us. He refused to let Hassan take me to the hospital because it was not a part of their family tradition. His wife had given birth to five children in the house in Shiraz naturally. And we were to maintain that tradition. Even Bibi didn't argue with them to force them to take me to hospital. I was terrified; I was in extreme pain. I could tell that Hassan didn't like the idea. He wanted to take me to the hospital, but because his brother was older and was like the father figure in the family, Hassan listened to him and nobody took me to the hospital. With all the bad things that Hassan always did to me, this time when he was about to do the right thing, his brother did not let him. He was the same brother who had told me that mice had stolen my gold. His decision was firmly made, and I had to give birth at home. The difference between me and his wife was that I was fourteen while she was in her thirties. My contractions went on for almost twenty-four hours. I begged for the doctors, but Hassan's brother kept denying me. They wouldn't even call my family. Maybe because they did not want them to argue or interfere about my giving birth at home, or they just wanted to surprise my family. I wasn't really upset that my mother was not there because she was in her own ninth month of pregnancy. And with all the pain I was in, I really could not see or hear anybody. They had called in a lady who had a lot of experience in child delivery, but no education at all. I was used to the pain and crying quietly. But this pain was far worse than any that I had ever felt before. I screamed and cried loudly and relentlessly the entire time. Hassan's brother turned up the living room radio so that the sound of my screams would not disturb Hassan and his brothers. I was in so much pain that I felt like I was losing my feet. Things were getting worse. They informed my family. I had no more energy and there was blood everywhere. I felt cold and weak. My contractions were finally over. It was time for me to push with all the strength that I had left after all the pain I had gone through. I was exhausted. I didn't have the strength to go through the process of pushing the child out of me. I screamed and pushed with all the power I had left in me. Finally, a baby came out. But I was so weak and lifeless that I couldn't even process that moment. That was when the most excruciating pain began. My small body gave birth to a ten-pound baby girl. She was so big that she came out along with my womb. My insides were completely pulled out and hanging from my body. I was almost dead. Everything was blurry, and I didn't even have the power to make a sound. I couldn't even ask to hold her, or see how beautiful she was. I was just fighting to keep my eyes open because I was afraid that if I closed them, I might never wake up again to see my daughter. The lady was frightened by the sight of my womb. She called for Hassan and his brother, and it took my dying body to convince his brother that I needed to go to the hospital. My uncle came along with my mother and grandmother as soon as they could. My uncle, as always, stood up for me. He ran up to me as soon as he saw me. "How could you do this? How could you!? Are you stupid? This is a child! I'll sue you. I'll sue all of you!" He created a big scene and screamed at Hassan and his brother. I could barely process what was happening around me. I would daze out some moments, and come back to reality with the sounds of my uncle's screams. "I'm taking her to the hospital! Go ahead, try and stop me. I don't care!" I was grateful for my uncle. My own father wouldn't stand up for me as much as he did. My own father didn't even show up. When we got to the hospital, doctors would not accept me. "Take her back to the place where they did this to her! You brought her here, so we could be responsible for her death?" doctors questioned. "She's going to die. You have been too late in bringing her here!" But my uncle didn't give up. He reminded them of who he was and of our family's importance in Shiraz. After long debates, the doctors finally agreed to hospitalize me under our own responsibility. The doctors discovered that my delivery should have been by cesarean surgery. My body was too petite to give birth to a ten-pound baby and I had needed to be under full supervision to give birth. The doctors made my uncle sign papers that he would be responsible for my life and to allow them to completely detach my womb from my body. Once I was in the operating room, they gave me blood and put me to sleep. The doctor felt bad that I was only fourteen, so they took the chance and tried to save my womb. They put my womb inside of me and sewed back everything in place. I woke up feeling very weak. I saw my entire family crowded around me except for Hassan and his family. My mother was telling all the relatives that it was because they were taking care of my baby. Maybe they didn't come because they were ashamed of what they had done to me. Maybe Hassan's brother would now realize that instead of turning the radio up, he should have listened to me and saved me.

I was in the hospital for a few days and it was hard for the nurses to stop my bleeding. They had to give me blood again and again. They told me that the stress of the pregnancy and the unusual way of giving birth had put too much pressure on my veins and given me varicose veins from my waist to my legs. The pain in the veins and my ripped-up body were killing me. But after all that I went through, I was lucky enough to be alive just for my daughter's sake. I wanted to be a good mother to her; nothing like my mother was to me. If God could give me the strength, then I would take care of her with all the love that I could give her. And that feeling kept me fighting, even more than before. I wanted to give her a life that I never had.

After the hospital discharged me, my uncle did not let Hassan and his brother take me to their place. There was a big fight at the hospital. Hassan and his brother didn't admit that they were wrong, and ordered me to go back home with them. My uncle once again stood up for me. My own mother disagreed with my uncle because she said I was Hassan's responsibility. "His family should take care of her; they should make her look like she did on her wedding day when we gave her away." I thought to myself that if they let Hassan take me with him, he would hit me very hard, because I was late, very late. I was away from home for almost a week. I was sure it did not matter to him that I was at the hospital; for him, late meant late. My injured body could not take any more kicks and my yellow face could not tolerate any slaps. Hassan and his family declared that if I went home with my family, I would never see my daughter again. My uncle didn't care what anybody said. He took me to my parents' house.

While I recovered at home, my uncle fought for me, and eventually Hassan brought my daughter to me. Hassan had named her Jaleh. The moment I held her in my arms, I fell in love. I loved her more than I had ever loved anybody or anything before. I instantly connected with her. As her little hands wrapped around my fingers, I knew that everything was going to be okay, as long as she was in this world. Jaleh was a beautiful, chubby girl with very white, silky skin and dark hair and big brown eyes. She looked like a mix of Bibi and Hassan and was very calm and peaceful. She was an angel.

I was getting my strength back little by little, and Hassan came to visit us once in a while and I was safe. I knew he could not harm me in front of my family. Even though my mother had three grandchildren, Mohammad and his sister, and my daughter, Jaleh, we all had to be happy for my mother and father because their new baby was on the way. My mother was happy again when her thirty-five-year-old self gave birth to her sixth child, a boy, exactly twenty-one days after my child's birth. I was still in my recovery period. My father had named him Nasir. Hundreds of relatives came to greet me and Mother at the same time with gifts. Amene and I were very embarrassed, mostly in front our husbands' families. My mother seemed very happy and my father was very proud.

After my pregnancy, we never went to Hassan's family house in Shiraz whenever we came from Bushehr again. We went directly to my parents', thanks to my uncle. This made summers in Shiraz much better, and I was safer from Hassan's beatings. But it became a routine for my mother to leave a year of her messy, dirty life for me to come back to every summer. I had to clean up after her, scrubbing germs from a filthy home. I had to cook for her and babysit; I practically became her live-in maid. But I never let Hassan find that out. It was easier to be a maid when you were safe from being beaten. I always did my mother's chores when Hassan went out to check on their properties, have fun with his family, and to cinemas and parks, enjoying his summer. Despite all this, I was far happier in my family's home, and was grateful for the change.

Chapter 12

People always say that life is short. I never witnessed time fly by, maybe because no matter how much time passed, my life stayed the same. It was always about routine, not only for me but also for everyone else around me.

My mother's routines were the most damaging to the people around her. She became pregnant again after giving birth to Nasir, and my parents couldn't be any happier about it.

I stayed at their house with Hassan until the end of that summer. I got my strength back and Jaleh was growing healthily and beautifully. We went back to Bushehr again. My parents were busy making babies and got used to the routine of me leaving for nine months. But to me, it was still forced, and I felt like I didn't belong in Bushehr.

I was in Bushehr when my mother gave birth to her seventh child, a boy. They had named him Ghafoor. In my mind, I thought of him as another victim, who probably had another tragic life ahead of him. Hassan hit me less after Jaleh was born, but he never stopped. He loved Jaleh so much that I was amazed. I never knew he had a heart that was able to love someone as deeply as he loved his daughter. Jaleh made me happy apart from making me value my life more. I tried to stand up against whatever adversity came my way. Jaleh changed my life. She gave me a strength that I never had before. The near-death experience I went through to have her was worth it. I started my days joyfully and passionately because of her. I started not to care if I was in Shiraz or Bushehr, in jail or in heaven, as long as I was with her.

As much as I loved to be in Shiraz, sometimes I was very happy that I was not with my family, especially when my mother was pregnant again. It was very shameful.

Hassan really wanted two children. But when I gave birth to Jaleh my body was damaged so much that the doctors had asked me to not have a second child until I was at least eighteen. Vein damage on my legs was so severe that I could easily see them all curled up under my skin. My body was never going to be the same. It was damaged. It needed a few years just to recover to a state where it would be able to manage to carry another child. I was more fragile than I had ever been before. But at the age of sixteen, I became pregnant again.

This time, Hassan cared more and took me to Shiraz every month so that I would regularly visit the hospital to ensure everything was going well. Some of his family members were still against it, but no one could stop Hassan. The doctors were worried because they didn't know if my womb could withstand having another baby in such a short period of time after my last pregnancy. Luckily, things were going well and during the nine months they reassured me that my baby was very healthy and was growing proportionately. The only pain that I had was from my varicose veins, which got worse as I got bigger and heavier each day. The veins in my legs were so swollen that I could barely stand because of extreme pain. Most of my pregnancy was spent on the road, traveling back and forth from Bushehr to Shiraz. The last few months of it I just stayed in Shiraz as per the doctor's recommendation.

Life was getting a little smoother for me. Hassan did not hit me during my second pregnancy, maybe because of the regular doctor visits. It would be too obvious, and because my health was so on the line I could have a miscarriage any minute. Hassan wanted a second baby more than anything, so he kept his hands off me. But, he still stopped talking to me every once in a while, as he always did. Hassan always told me to tell people that he and I wanted another daughter. I had never thought of the gender of my child before, but I made sure I told friends and family that we wanted a baby girl. But Hassan didn't actually want a daughter again, I assumed; he wanted a son. He just didn't want people to pity us if the second baby turned out to be a girl again. It was very important for wives to give birth to sons. For some families, having a daughter was considered nothing but a burden and sorrow. It made me think that maybe my father was sorry that he had three daughters and got rid of us as soon as he could. The idea was that boys could go to work and take over family businesses while daughters were just another mouth to feed. Girls were also considered to be more difficult to raise, and took much more effort and discipline. I loved my daughter and I did not mind having another one. Girl or boy, my child was a gift from God and I was simply thankful.

When I went into labor, I was taken to the hospital without hesitation. This time I gave birth like a human being and not like an animal. It was far easier than the first time. I wish I was taken to the hospital when I was giving birth to Jaleh too. Then I would not have experienced that excruciating pain in my life, of which the memories would be with me forever. Soon I gave birth to a beautiful baby girl, who Hassan had named Laleh. Laleh was a normal 6.6lb girl with darker skin, curly black hair, and brown eyes. As soon as they gave Laleh to me to hold, I knew I had given birth to a warrior. She was going to conquer the world. "Be strong, baby. I got you. I got you for life," I said to her. I loved her with all my heart. I was completely happy having two daughters, but many of my relatives felt sorry for me. They said that they'd pray for our third child to be a son. Hassan was right. People were nosy and rude. Hassan was very happy having two kids and he was fine with them being girls. He didn't want any more children because he wanted to make sure he paid equal attention, with lots of love and discipline, to both his daughters. He felt that it would be harder with more kids. Before I had given birth, Hassan said to me, "It's okay if it's a girl. No matter what the gender is, two children are plenty. We'll be a complete family." I agreed with him. I thought about all my siblings and myself and how little attention my mother paid to us. But I began to worry that Hassan was hiding his true emotions. What if Hassan really wanted to have boys? I started to think about giving Hassan a son; I wanted to make him happy. I just wasn't sure what to do.

The same year that my second child was born Amene gave birth to her third child, a boy. In the meantime, my parents did not forget about Masume and she was forced to marry at the age of fourteen. Masume had hoped that after what had happened to Amene and me, my parents would let her study. But of course, to my parents, girls were just another mouth to feed and Masume had to go. I was glad that my parents only had three daughters among all their children.

Masume became pregnant right after she got married. And of course, my mother had to feel young and show others how she had no problems getting pregnant, just like her fourteen-year-old daughter. So my mother gave birth to her eighth child, a baby boy named Isa. Masume gave birth to a boy, two weeks after my mother. Our relatives constantly humiliated my sisters and me about having brothers the same age as our own children. They were sarcastic and practically made fun of us. We got bullied because of the shame our parents put us through. My mother couldn't see that nobody was impressed with her ability to have kids. They talked behind her back. It was slowly degrading her reputation. None of us three daughters could hold our heads up and look into our relatives' eyes.

By this time, my brother Zein had gotten his high school diploma and wanted to continue his education in America. He always cared about studying and never cared about what our parents were doing. Now it was his time and he wanted to leave, to study and make us all proud. For a while, he was gathering all the documents that were needed to leave the country. He was the pride of the family, and we were so happy for him. It was a decision my mother was happy about because sending her child to the United States for education really improved her reputation. It was a big deal and not many people would send their kids to foreign countries for education.

My mother had kids of all ages. She had newborns, toddlers, teenagers, adults, and married ones with sons-in-law and grandchildren. It was complicated to keep up with them all. My father was more like an object, a wall or a book or something, a mere decoration of sorts. He was never really there for any of his children, and even when he was there we could not feel his presence. The ages were so different that my mother could neither keep track of all her kids nor made the effort to. Every time my mother gave birth to a new child, she cared less and less about her other children because she was too busy dealing with her pregnancy or taking care of her newborns. My mother did not look after my brother Ebrahim at all. Zein was always respected by my mother because he was her first son, but Ebrahim was left alone all by himself amid all our marriages and problems, and then Nasir was born and then Ghafoor and then Isa. He went wild without any supervision. He was a teenager and because my mother paid more attention to the younger kids in the house, Ebrahim began to do anything that he wanted without my mother's knowing. I couldn't blame him. Every teenager would do the same and go a little wrong, but Ebrahim made some very bad choices. He started getting into the habit of sneaking out of the house in the middle of the night, stealing the car, and driving to meet his friends when he did not even have a driver's license. God knows the things Ebrahim did in the middle of the night, but everyone knew they were not good things. Ebrahim even started doing drugs and gambling. He went out so much that he was barely home, and he always returned high and drunk. My mother only began to realize that Ebrahim was getting out of hand when he was already too far out of reach. Things got worse every day. Zein was in the United States when my mother was pregnant with her ninth child. She knew that Ebrahim was long gone and she should have stopped thinking about her youth and done something about him. But nothing really mattered to my mother but herself and her desires and her joy and her passions. I don't think she ever worried about Ebrahim overdosing, or his leaving one day and never coming back. She focused more on having a relaxing, stress-free ninth pregnancy.

When something difficult came into my mother's life, her goal was to not stress herself out. She'd always say that problems brought her depression back, so she'd focus on not necessarily solving anything, but just disposing of her problems and getting them out of her way, so that her life could remain easy and simple. Ebrahim was neck-deep in a pool of his own mistakes. He was, at that time, the problem in my father and mother's life. If she really cared, she would not have let him get in the position that he was in. He was only seventeen and broken, a victim of neglect. My mother realized that she had to do something when her reputation was on the line. People started to notice how Ebrahim was turning into an improvident teenager, so they started talking and it was making my mother look bad. She began to realize that everyone in our family blamed her for Ebrahim's behavior. They kept saying how could she bring four more kids into this world when the first five was so scattered. So for the people to say that she cared, my mother started to try to fix Ebrahim somehow. But it was already too late. Ebrahim was like a wild buffalo that was hard to tame. He was long gone. That's when my mother decided to do what she always did when she no longer wanted to be responsible for a child; she started trying to find him a wife. My brother was not ready for marriage. He had so much to learn, so much to fix. He was not fit to be a husband. My mother and father were going to ruin someone's daughter and hand her over to a depraved seventeen-year-old boy. It was more unusual for a boy to marry young than a girl, so it was hard to find him a wife. My mother usually went to rich families for marriage, but since Ebrahim was seventeen and many people knew he was into drugs and alcohol, it was hard to find him a wife from a decent family. So my mother started looking at lower-class families. There was one family, who had next to no money, who had agreed to give their daughter to Ebrahim.

The bride's father was an old, very kind man who had a small men's sewing shop for handmade pants, eleven kids, and a tiny house. He was a very supportive father who worked very hard and was sending his children one by one to university. Education was very important to him. He was a really good father. The family had an eighteen-year-old girl named Mariam. She was a very beautiful, intelligent, and sweet girl. She was a year older than Ebrahim. She had already graduated from high school and had got admission into university. She declined my mother's marriage proposal to Ebrahim because she knew that a husband would get in the way of her education. This family was my mother's last opportunity to wed Ebrahim, and she couldn't bear rejection, especially when she had already made up her mind. In my parents' minds, Mariam would rebuild Ebrahim. This family had no idea that Ebrahim had many unsolved issues. My parents did not care about Mariam's dreams of studying. My parents went to their home several times and Mariam said no. They talked to her father and he said it would be Mariam's decision. He respected her wishes. I always looked at this man and thought to myself that this father barely had a sixth-grade education, but his dream for his kids was for them to grow up as teachers, engineers, and doctors. My father, on the other hand, was a highly educated person and yet he ruined our lives and never asked for our opinions or what our wishes were.

To get her way, my mother had to convince Mariam somehow. She told Mariam that she need not worry about the university that she had already been accepted to. My mother, however, had different plans: When Mariam married my brother Ebrahim, Zein would send out an invitation, and my parents would send them both to America. Mariam could continue her studies there as well; my parents would take care of the expenses until they graduated. For a girl whose life revolved around studying and who hoped to achieve something from education, my mother's words sounded like a dream come true. Mariam accepted my mother's offer because she knew Ebrahim was from a wealthy family and they could afford to send them to America, so she decided to marry Ebrahim, according to all those conditions.

After all the battles, my parents won, and the wedding was going to happen. My pregnant mother was hosting her son's wedding. Mariam looked very beautiful and happy. She had the American dream. She was a beautiful girl, very attractive. Ebrahim loved her from the minute he laid his eyes on her. The love he had for her made him quit all the mischief he had done and gotten attached to in his life. Mariam was like his savior who turned him into a man nobody thought he would become in such a short time. My mother's plan worked to save Ebrahim, but at the price of destroying Mariam's life. Mariam helped Ebrahim to graduate and get his diploma. She encouraged him very kindly with love and supported him so that he could study hard. Finally, she did it.

The time came for my mother to ask Zein to send them an invitation to go to America, as she had promised. She played around for a few months on diploma's alibi and again played them with the excuse of waiting for the invitation. She gave birth to her ninth child in this huge messy time, a son named Musa. A year passed, and Mariam was living in a room in my parents' house with Ebrahim, constantly waiting to go to America like my mother had promised. But she was a smart girl. Deceit and manipulation were always my mother's way of achieving her goals. Mariam realized all my mother's lies. Ebrahim really did believe my mother. He really thought our parents were going to send them to America. Mariam never blamed him for my mother's lies.

Mariam was a strong girl and she decided to go to the university that she got accepted to as a nurse and worked on sending Ebrahim to university as well. But in my family, girls were not supposed to have a bright future at all. They had no right to be educated, maybe because my mother could not compete an education, so all the girls who surrounded her had to be forbidden too.

My parents decided that they did not want Mariam to continue her education at all. Once again, my mother managed to crush the hopes and dreams of an innocent person who she had lied to. My mother, with only one lie, ruined Mariam's life. She changed her destiny completely, and left her with a broken heart on a dead-end road. Mariam could have gone to university and studied and become someone special, but she was not allowed to.

My parents were the ones who fed them, as Mariam and Ebrahim had no money and no place to go. They were very young, and her family was poor and was unable to help, even if they wanted to. My parents laid the best possible trap for Mariam, a thick, sticky web of lies that would make her a prisoner in one corner of their house forever. To my parents, Mariam was just someone who would rescue their son, so people would stop talking about my mother. My parents achieved their goals and Ebrahim was back from the path of deterioration. In their minds, they were kind enough to shelter them and feed them, and every day my mother made sure to remind Mariam that she was from a poor family and how she got lucky enough to step into this family.

Our family was growing into a knotted, snarled clew of silk, impossible to untie, where the only solution was to burn the silk.

Chapter 13

I USED TO OBEY HASSAN FOR FEAR OF HIS ABUSE, BUT mistreatment was his hobby whether I did right or wrong. I realized that I was standing on a pathway to my dreams, and everybody knew he was obstructing my way, keeping me from moving forward. For a long time, I stood still, letting them stop me. But the more I waited, strength grew inside of me. It made me into a bowling ball, and I was ready to knock them all down.

Hassan always hit me because I loved to dress up and take care of myself. No matter how much he hit me at night, I'd get up the next morning and dress up again, even fancier than the day before. It was who I wanted to be, and I refused to let him stop me. The repetition began to bore him, and he eventually stopped hitting me for how I dressed. I was beginning to really learn Hassan's ways. He was a wild horse and I focused on trying to tame him.

What I really wanted in life was to continue my education. I had stopped after sixth grade when I had to marry Hassan. Now that I had a married life, Hassan didn't want me to go to school. He had no particular reason; he just didn't want me to do anything that I wanted to do. I sometimes think that if I had told him I hated school and never wanted to go, then he'd have forced me to go. Every time I asked Hassan if I could take classes, he'd beat me and stop talking to me for weeks on end. I grew tired of it. All he did was hit me whether I did right or wrong. Just as I dressed up the way that I liked, I decided to do everything that I wanted no matter what Hassan said. I didn't want to ask his permission anymore. All his beatings just made me thick-skinned. I was a woman who could stand on her own, and I was determined to attend school. I felt so empowered going against his will that I signed up for night school because I was married. The law wouldn't allow married women to attend normal schools because they believed we'd corrupt the virgins.

"What didn't you understand when I said NO?" Hassan had found out that I had signed up for night school. Although I stood against his wishes with my actions, I never spoke back to him. I couldn't change anything with my words. He would only beat me harder, so I always respected him. "You can't go! I won't allow it!" he shouted, and of course he grabbed me and beat me until he felt better. After that, he stopped talking to me. It was predictable, nothing but routine. I went to school as soon as all the paperwork was done. My classes started at five in the afternoon when Hassan was working in his father's store, and they finished at nine, which was the store's closing time. As much as I tried to get home fast, I always came home a few minutes after his return, and Hassan beat me harder every time. One time when I got home around twenty minutes after him, he nearly killed me. I was unconscious on the floor, fighting for my life. He pulled at my long hair and dragged me down all the stairs toward the main door. He was going to throw me out of the house because in his mind only whores came home that late at night, even though he knew I was at school. His brothers and Bibi always came to my rescue when Hassan took things this far. After all those years of abuse, the only thing that hurt me was my girls running around me, screaming and crying and frightened as Hassan pounded my flesh. He didn't care that our kids were around. He wanted to shame me in front of them. He wanted them to know that I deserved it. But my daughters were never ashamed of me. They never believed that I deserved such abuse.

The expression on Jaleh's and Laleh's faces and the tears in their eyes shattered my shield of strong will, as if it were made of glass. They would hug me and hold me away from Hassan, as if they wanted to protect me. I was supposed to protect my daughters, but they felt like they needed to protect me. Hassan was too blind to see the fear in his own children's eyes, so he just ignored them and continued hitting me. They were old enough to understand what was happening, and I was old enough to not let Hassan put me down. Even after all that, I went to school the next evening. Soon, he grew tired of hitting me. He knew that I would not give up and listen, so he slowly stopped, and eventually I won the fight like I knew I would.

Years passed, and he even helped me with my studies and homework like he was the one who had asked me to go back to school. I stood up for my going to school, and soon I began to stand up for other things that I wanted for me and my daughters' sake.

I was the only woman in Hassan's family who went back to school. Now that I was doing very well at school and was almost eighteen, I was anxious to learn to drive a car and get my driver's license. None of my jaaris knew how to drive even though they were years older than me. I also knew that Hassan would not support me in getting a driver's license.

But I knew him well. He told me that it was not necessary for me to have a driver's license and I refused to listen to him. I got a driving booklet and started to study for the test. Hassan started to hit me again. It was like he never learned that hitting me would not get his point across. I was going to do what I wanted regardless of the pain he put me through. He thought that abuse was the solution to everything. And once again, he was wrong. When I passed the written driving test, and it was time to do the actual driving test, he taught me how to drive and let me use his car for the test.

He always drove up-to-date and fancy-looking cars, and didn't really like people driving his cars but he let me. I took the test, passed it on my first try, and got my driver's license. No matter how much I pretended to look brave, I was always very afraid of him deep down.

Being able to drive helped with a lot of other things that I wanted to do. Hassan let me borrow his car once or twice a week and gave me a good amount of money once a month to spend on me and my daughters. I used to gather all my sisters-in-law, Bibi, and the kids and go shopping and to the theater, get ice cream, and have lots of fun together as we all lived like sisters all those years. I bought Jaleh and Laleh beautiful dresses and cute clothes too. Since Bibi taught me how to sew, I bought beautiful fabrics and made very nice dresses for my lovely girls and myself. I had to use an old sewing machine that we had, and I had to spin its handle to sew.

My girls always looked neat and fashionable. They were very polite and great in school. Since Hassan saw how much I loved fashion and sewing, he bought me the most expensive modern sewing machine available at the time and sent me to a special class to learn how to use it. Whenever new things came out, Hassan bought them for us so we could stay updated and live easier and more comfortably. He stopped hitting me and he worked hard and had a great habit of saving money. He started buying me jewelry and made me very happy and proud. But his attitude and the silent treatments continued.

Life was getting a little smoother. Hassan cared about the future of our girls and his retirement. He knew we would not live forever in Bushehr because I never got used to it, and I always felt like a visitor. As an investment for our future welfare and convenience, Hassan bought a good two-story house in a nice area in Shiraz, with a total of six rooms including two large living rooms and dining rooms, as well as two modern kitchens. We spent the summers in Shiraz in our own home. The house was new and very pretty and we all were very excited to be there. It felt good going to my own house and not my mother's. We soon became friends with our neighbors. So many nice families lived in that alley.

Our trips back to Bushehr were getting better since the government had started to pave and widen the road. This allowed us to travel to Shiraz more often because the traveling time was reduced to just five hours. Everything was getting better and my girls were growing into very well-mannered, beautiful little dolls. Sometimes, when he wanted to discipline them, Hassan would hit Laleh and Jaleh, but not as violently as he used to hit me. The girls were very afraid of him, but they loved him very much because they knew how much he loved them and cared for them.

Hassan often had to travel to Shiraz only if it was just for a day to check up on his family business. We never joined him since it was a long trip. Hassan used to leave early in the morning and return the next day.

One day, Hassan did not return home when he was supposed to. My brother-in-law told me that Hassan had called and said he had to stay a little longer. It really did not seem normal, but I believed him because we only had one home phone line in the main rooms of the house, which my brother-in-law always answered. A few days passed, and Hassan came home, but without his brand-new car, which we had bought just a few weeks earlier. He was fine, completely healthy, and he explained that he was involved in a very serious accident when he was almost to Shiraz. It was a two-way road, and one careless driver was trying to pass another car on a curve of the spiral road. By the time Hasan saw the car, it was too late and they smashed into each other hard. He had pain in both his hands and one foot and whiplash had hurt his back. Those pains stayed with him always.

His car was crushed in such a way that he said everyone who saw him walk out of that car was amazed and kept saying it was a miracle that he was even alive. There was no car insurance in those days and the car was a total loss, but all we cared about was his being safe, and we were grateful that he had survived.

Chapter 14

Amene gave birth to her fourth child, and now she had two sons and two daughters. Her youngest daughter was born with mental retardation. Masume gave birth to two more sons nine months apart and now she had three sons. Every time I was at a family gathering, everybody's questions were: Wouldn't you like to have a son too? Why don't you try to have another child? Oh, can't you become pregnant anymore? Is it because of your varicose veins? Are you scared about your next baby being a girl too?

Hassan never paid any attention to what people said, but it did affect me. I asked Hassan so many times to try and have another child, but Hassan always refused and had many good reasons for it. He said we were happy and growing in life and had passed all the stages of taking care of little ones, and starting all over again would be very difficult. "Kids need a future and parents' support. We have to supervise them and walk with them through their lives. If we have another child, the age difference between them would be too much, and then we'd have to put all our attention toward the youngest one and the girls would be left behind," he had said. To me, no matter what he said, it felt like the right thing to do. In my mind, I felt like he wanted a son too and he just wouldn't admit it. I felt like I was missing something since everybody kept telling me that I should have a son. I just really wanted a baby boy and eventually Hassan agreed to try. I thought a boy could fill up the emptiness in my life.

I became pregnant at the age of twenty-four with my third child. I was very happy and Hassan seemed happy as well. I was going to be twenty-five and my daughters would be eleven and nine on my due date. We were all very excited. Because of my varicose veins, I had to go to Shiraz once a month for checkups. When I was six months' pregnant, the doctors did not let me travel back to Bushehr and I stayed with my parents so they could look after me because Hassan had to go back to Bushehr, as he was teaching, and my daughters had to go to school. Every Thursday Hassan drove back to Shiraz with our girls, so I could see them and the next day, that is, on Friday, they would drive back to Bushehr to start school on Saturday morning. It was not easy for any of us, but we all looked forward to having a new addition to our family. My brother Zein graduated from university and was about to come back to Iran from the United States after four long years of studying. We all had missed him so much, and could not wait to see him.

My parents bought the most beautiful two-story mansion at that time, which was built by American designers and architects. It had eighteen rooms, with a beautiful open-concept ballroom and classic stairs at the side of the entrance. All the floors were covered with white granite. The house was painted in all white, with many beautiful windows and columns. The house had a big front yard with a nice large swimming pool. The house was really a dream house for many and was in a good neighborhood. Everybody in Shiraz called it the White House. Nowadays these kinds of houses are in plenty, but back then it was unique architecture.

My mother spent all the money on her mansion, which she had built years ago on one of her lands not far from Shiraz. It became like a cottage where we used to go at the end of the week for a little fun. But she always dreamed of a huge, beautiful house, and the White House finally made her dream come true.

We wear all very happy for them, and they moved in before Zein's arrival. Ebrahim and Mariam moved into a room in the new house as well because they had no other choice. My mother completely put them out of her mind and they were just there dumbfounded and trapped. At that point in my mother's life, Ebrahim and Mariam's lives were simply destroyed. There were also my mother and father's extra four little boys who were just growing up in the middle of a crowded family with many issues. My mother only cared about one child out of her nine and that child was Zein.

When Zein came back almost a hundred family members and friends showed up at the airport and my parents threw the biggest party they'd ever had to welcome him. It was a splendid and magnificent party with a perfect dinner.

Back then, there were women whose jobs were to help families to find suitable wives or husbands for their sons and daughters. These women were called matchmakers, who would listen to all their clients' expectations and information. Then they would talk to a suitable family and arrange a time for the families to meet in the form of a friendly tea party that everyone would attend except for the fathers. This gave an opportunity for the bride- and groom-to-be to meet each other and see if they liked each other. If everything went well, the fathers would attend the second visit. But for Amene and me, times were different, and we never met our husbands first.

As was the tradition, my mother, Amene, Masume, Mariam, and I with Zein of course started going to the houses of the families who had girls for him to choose as a wife. Zein was looking for an educated, beautiful girl close to his age from a well-known and rich family.

Poor Mariam, she was supposed to become educated and push Ebrahim for the same. But my parents did not let her because it was shameful for the girls in my family to study. However, now that Zein deserved an educated girl, my mother forgot about all her beliefs and started searching for the same. Every family we went to had good houses and was wealthy, but not as wealthy as my parents, and Mariam had to witness all of this as my mother dragged her along to show her how unfortunate she was. My mother enjoyed reminding her that she came from a lower-class family. Mariam was getting more and more skinny, weak, sad, and quiet as the days went by. My mother never noticed or didn't care to notice. Finally, Zein chose his future wife who had a degree and came from a successful family.

I was in the last month of pregnancy and we were getting closer to my due date. Hassan was very caring and supportive at the time and I could see the happiness shining in his eyes. My girls were very patient, and they never complained.

Back then, you had to wait until your baby was born to know the gender. As much as I prayed for a healthy child, in my heart I wanted a son. Hassan never talked about wanting a son and only prayed for me and the child's health.

One autumn night at 9:00 p.m., I gave birth to a healthy and most wonderful baby boy. I couldn't believe it. He was a dream come true. I was fine during the labor and nothing went wrong. All our relatives congratulated me on having a boy, I felt so relieved and accomplished. My father called Hassan in Bushehr and gave him the good news. He drove to Shiraz with the girls the next morning. The girls took a few days off from school to be with me and their baby brother. Even though Hassan never mentioned wanting a son, I could tell how happy he was and how proud he was holding our baby boy in his arms. The moment I saw my baby, I knew his name had to be Arash, based on the legendary archer. Jaleh and Laleh loved Arash, and those days were some of the most cheerful days of our lives.

My parents' house was full of happiness and gatherings for Zein's wedding. Everybody was doing something to help with the arrangements and my parents had a big ceremony and gave lots of expensive gifts to the new bride. It was easy to see the difference between Ebrahim's and Zein's weddings.

Ebrahim and Mariam never got those kinds of gifts from my parents. Ebrahim and Mariam were both very kind. They were never jealous or bitter. They never complained about how much better my mother treated Zein. It was always hurtful for me to witness the unfairness, and not be able to do anything about it.

Zein lived in the White House as well, but Mother gave them a whole story to themselves, the second level of the house. They had their privacy, to live and cook privately and be with the family when they felt like it, but Mariam had to be with my family twenty-four seven and never had her privacy respected. She had to eat with my parents and help with cooking and cleaning, washing the dishes, and practically raising my mother's four little sons.

At that time, Iran was governed by King Pahlavi, and Iranian people wanted more freedom and democracy. The Iranian government was in a shaky situation and people were starting to join different political groups. It was the Iranian revolution. They started with small rallies and the king's army killed people to stop the revolts. As people got angrier, the rallies started to become more crowded. The entire nation was in chaos and there was no security or safety. Every day, more people were killed. But people did not give up and the rallies were attended by millions and it was getting more difficult for the government to control the madness.

Soon the government announced a strict curfew from 9:00 p.m. to 7:00 a.m. Schools were closed, and Hassan and his brothers closed down the stores for safety. Anarchy and disorder spread vastly, and the country went out of control. Hassan and his brothers stayed at home and did not go to work for a few months.

During these hard times, Arash was growing cuter and more adorable every day, and everybody enjoyed his company, especially Jaleh and Laleh who volunteered to do everything for him. Even though they were years older than Arash, they never got jealous of him nor felt like they were left behind.

During the day, if the town was quiet we would go out for important tasks, like Arash's vaccines or supplies.

One night, Arash was burning with a fever and as hard as we tried, we were not able to bring down his temperature, and we had to take him to the emergency room. The curfew started at 9:00 p.m., and it was already past midnight. We could not wait until morning; my baby needed help. Because the army was harsher on men, we decided that I'd take Arash to the hospital with Laleh. We all were very scared, but we started the car and drove out of the house, hoping for the best. In less than a second, the army stopped the car, but when they saw a woman with an ill infant in a child's lap, they escorted our car to the hospital. Doctors told me if we had waited until morning, my son would have suffocated due to laryngitis. Thank God we had gone to the hospital on time.

Six months had passed since the closing of all government administrations and businesses. The revolution came to an end and they had finally tasted victory by changing the government. Everything seemed to go back to normal to some extent. But life only got worse for wealthy people. The new government occupied the rich people's properties and confiscated them. Whoever was more involved with the royal family before the revolution was executed without a proper trial and court procedures. They arrested one of Hassan's brothers and Hassan's family had to pay a huge ransom. We were all thankful that he came home safe and was not executed. Everybody in our family was in danger and was losing properties as well. My father shut down the magazine and school right away and stayed at home and hid away from all the mess. Iran went underwent a different kind of bedlam and life was getting more difficult in different ways.

In the midst of it all, Amene gave birth to her fifth child

who was a boy, and Mariam gave birth to her first child, a boy.

Traveling on the roads was very dangerous as guns were widely available. Some people abused the new changes and closed the roads and robbed those who passed. Different political parties were fighting against one another to win the battle. People were very afraid of a civil war happening and the disaster that would ensue.

Chapter 15

THE ISLAMIC REVOLUTION, IN WHICH THE ISLAMIC REPUBLIC wanted to overthrow Iran's monarchy completely changed the lives of the Iranian people forever. Before Khomeini, the leader of the Islamic republic took over Iran's monarchy, pre-revolutionary opposition groups were created. The four main groups were constitutionalism, Marxism, Islamism, and communism. These main categories had more subgroups, all opposed by Khomeini. These groups used to lead big projects that teenagers followed.. Some of the projects were as foul as assassinating other leaders of the oppositions. But much of the time, because of these groups, people would start protests and vandalize the cities. Because there was a fear of these groups, and everyone who was a part of them was a threat to the revolution, the Islamic republic declared war and heavily cracked down on the opposition.

People were still struggling with the new rules and political conflicts, when Iraq invaded Iran. We had just returned from Shiraz to start a new school year in Bushehr. The kids had a few days left to get ready, and we all were at home when we heard Iraq's fighter jets barraging the streets with machine guns and bombing. We were terrified. I never feared for my children's life as much as I did when I heard those bombs. My kids were crying. Hassan and his brothers were trying to figure out how to handle the situation. We were all just running around like crazy and did not know what to do or where to go. The new government announced that we were at war with Iraq, and every Iranian was in shock. The political parties were still killing one another and now a foreign country took advantage of the instability and started a war. It was very sad and terrifying news. From that day, all the south of Iran was in danger and became a war zone. The government cut the electricity of the entire south from 5:00 p.m. until morning so that the enemy jets would not see the civilized areas easily. From just before dark until morning we all gathered in one of the rooms at night with all my brothers-in-law and sisters-in-laws, Bibi, and the kids They closed all the stores before dark and we were not allowed to even light a candle. We all slept in that room and every time we heard attacks, we all ran into the basement. Life during the day went back to normal after a week, the kids went to school, and in the evenings the entire city turned into a ghost town. Months passed, and we were still living that way. People started to cover all the windows to light a lantern and at least be able to see one another.

In the midst of the war, I found out that I was pregnant. It was a very shocking for both Hassan and me. It was unexpected, and we did not know what to do. It was no time for a baby. Jaleh was fourteen and we felt so embarrassed to have a child again. When we announced our pregnancy, Jaleh was the first one who blamed us for the mistake that we made not caring about the age difference between the kids and the political and economic mayhem. She was right, and we knew it, but there was nothing we could do. For a while, she was mad at us and did not talk much. I remembered the damage my parents caused to us older kids by having too many kids, and now we were doing it to our kids too. We accepted the blame and went on with our lives. There was nothing I could do. I was ashamed.

With my being pregnant, the country's being at war, and small political groups' being secretly active, I felt very bad, confused. Thinking about the poor little innocent baby on the way, and my fifteen-year-old who needed so much help and guidance made me feel miserable. I felt like I was betraying my kids.

Any person suspected of involvement in any political group was arrested. The consequences were executions without even a proper trial and actual proof. They would either kill the people they suspected to be group followers on the spot, or after they had spent some time imprisoned. The main issue was that the people who followed those groups were mostly under the age of twenty, which put a lot of young lives at risk. They followed those groups out of no knowledge and mostly made childish and wrong decisions. They just wanted change, but didn't really know what they were fighting for.

A cloud of fright and worry hung above the heads of many parents in Iran, including ours. Jaleh was a teenager and we were worried and scared that she might join one of the groups because it was beginning to become a trend among the teens, although I knew Jaleh was different than other kids her age. She was highly intelligent, beautiful, and mature. Even though she had turned fifteen, she appeared to be twenty, which tempted several men to marry her. I am not just saying that because I'm her mother, it was something everybody saw in her. At every party or family gathering we went to, at least one family would approach Hassan and me for permission for their son to take Jaleh's hand in marriage. But no matter how rich or handsome the boy was, Jaleh said no without hesitation. She was not the type of girl who was interested in marriage or love. She was more interested in reading books, studying hard, and reaching her goal of becoming an educated woman. That had been her passion ever since she was a kid. And of course, she felt marriage would get in the way of her dreams. Hassan and I were very proud of her and we supported her lifestyle wholeheartedly. But as soon as the revolution started, Jaleh's habits of reading began to become an issue. We noticed that the books Jaleh was reading were based on the different opposition groups. The fact that she was even reading about them worried Hassan because he thought if she knew more about them, she would become more curious and would be tempted to join one of them. Jaleh reassured us that all she was doing was learning about what was going on in Iran, and researching to find out more about the groups and the kind of people who followed them. Hassan feared that the research she was doing was actually for her, to see what group fit her best to join. No matter what Hassan and I told her, she continued reading about them. Even if we knew that she would not completely join the groups, we feared that when she went to school, somebody would find out she was researching about them, and they would report her. It would end with her being imprisoned or even being executed. We feared getting a phone call telling us that Jaleh was arrested or had been killed like the rest of the teenagers who followed those groups.

It was summer when we were in the middle of dealing with Jaleh's need of forbidden knowledge and the war when I gave birth to the dearest and the sweetest boy, whom I named Ashkan. He was such an adorable baby who brought a lot of joy into our family.

Devastating news spread through our family that completely brought back the fear for our kids to the surface. The government had killed Hassan's cousin because she was allegedly a part of an opposition group. The news made Hassan and me realize that Jaleh's research was more of a big deal than we had thought. Although hearing about all those young girls and boys dying was overwhelming and extremely saddening, it was even more devastating to hear that a person we knew was executed. This left Hassan with no choice but to confront Jaleh one last time.

For months, Hassan banned Jaleh from reading political books. But she still continued. "It's just research," Jaleh said, over and over again. There was something about her words that was not convincing, and her reason was not good enough. It was hard to understand why she was so insistent about knowing so much about the groups. Even the books that she was reading were banned and if anyone reported us the government would execute her.

"You have researched enough, Jaleh! You have researched

more than enough actually!" Hassan started to raise his voice. He gave me a look and walked out of the room. I knew that look; this was the final straw for Hassan. I wanted to believe my daughter, but it was very hard. With everything going on and the people around us dying, I didn't understand why she wouldn't just stop. I took one look at Jaleh and followed Hassan out of the room. There was nothing I could really say. For months we had said all that we could but nothing had convinced her. When I followed Hassan out of the room, he said that he was tired of trying to convince her to stop. Nothing was working, and it was time that we took proper action as parents to keep her from ruining her own life. "She's fifteen, she's pretty, men constantly ask for her hand in marriage... It's time, Najma. It's time. We need to get her out of these stupid teenage behaviors. She's trying to get herself killed. She needs to start acting like a woman now," Hassan said to me. I never wanted an early marriage for my daughter, but his words sounded reasonable; they sounded right. I did not know what else to do but agree. Our daughter's life was at risk because of her irrationality and it was up to Hassan and me to keep her from doing anything stupid with her life. Besides, she was not that young. She was fifteen.

Breaking the news to her was not easy. She kept complaining about how we were obliterating her future by making her marry young. She did not see that we were helping her out by steering her away from a wrong path that she was taking. She asked, "And what about my education? You are going to throw that in the dumpster just like that?" We knew that her education meant a lot to her, and it was not that we did not care. We were her parents. We were proud of the smart choices that she made for her future, but her careless decisions and immaturity toward the revolution made us realize the most important thing, which was her life.

So we told her that she could continue her education after she got married, and that marriage would not stop her but keep her safe. She begged and pleaded with Hassan and me to understand. She even reminded me of how I was forced to be married young, and I never wanted my daughters to marry at an early age. We wanted them to finish their education and fall in love and choose their future husbands on their own. Unfortunately, everything was going wrong, and the control of our lives was out of our hands. We were simply lost.

Chapter 16

Everything in our lives was a complicated mess. I had two young sons who needed me in a completely different way, and my two teenage daughters who also needed me more than ever. They were confused and were left behind unintentionally, but they never complained. Taking care of two little boys was not easy, and it occupied my days and nights. Somehow life had gotten out of hand very fast. I was very busy with the boys and my girls had to help a lot with their brothers and I was still studying, and I didn't realize how much pressure I had put on them at the time. They were very kind and sweet and never refused to help. Looking back now, I feel like I should have stopped going to school and had devoted more time to them. But I guess being in Hassan's prison for years and then being released, made me want to do everything for myself, everything I was denied for years. All that made me forget about the real purpose of my life: my children.

We gave Jaleh the opportunity to choose among the guys who proposed, something my mother never allowed her daughters. Hassan and I assumed that eventually Jaleh would realize that we were really doing all of that for her own good. Instead, as the days passed she felt more betrayed and shattered. I did not want to see my own daughter in a state of mind in which she felt as though her life was unfair, but I just told myself that she was blinded by a teenage mind that lacked the ability to tell the difference between right and wrong. I knew that Jaleh was a strong girl, but her strength was working against her future. She started confronting us on a regular basis. She kept triggering the same argument over and over again about how she did not want to live the same life that I had lived and how I was doing to her what my mother had done to me. Her words did speak to me, but I was forced to be married as a kid. She was a beautiful grown young woman. It was different. I never saw my future husband. She was smart, and she had every right to be able to continue her education and I really wanted that for her. I believed that no girl should be pushed to get married, but times had changed. The revolution and war made it a necessity. Hassan was being logical; making her marry seemed was the only right thing to do to keep her safe and alive. She argued but it did not change our minds; the decision had been made. As we were from a recognized family in Shiraz, as soon as people heard that we were willing to marry our daughter, close relatives and friends stepped in.

Jaleh had many options, but nobody seemed to impress her. It was more the fact that she did not want to be impressed in the first place, but that wasn't going to stop Hassan from finding a husband for her. He decided to be the one to choose since she would not.

We came across a lot of wonderful, wealthy families that seemed great. We searched among the long list of families that wanted our daughter's hand in marriage. After a short while of searching, we came across a family that stood out so much that they blurred out every other option we had in mind, and shined.

Their son Reza was a very handsome man. He was twenty-one years old, tall, masculine, attractive, and most of all, smart. He had just returned home from America where he had graduated with a major in civil engineering, specializing in bridges and buildings. He had received his degree at the age of nineteen. His intelligence stood out to both Hassan and me. Everything about him was brilliant, everything except for one thing. His family was much more religious than ours. We followed our faith, but Reza's family took it to a different level. I kept telling Hassan that we should keep looking for other options because their level of religious practice did not fit ours, and that Jaleh would be forced to live a lifestyle that she was not used to. But something about Reza had caught Hassan's eye, which blinded Hassan of all his other flaws, and Hassan convinced us that he was the one for Jaleh.

Hassan began to replace Reza's problems with "what ifs" and "maybes." "What if she changes him?" Hassan asked. "What if she tones down his religiousness?" Hassan was lying to himself.

"Nobody can change anybody; I tried changing you for years," I responded. I knew that Reza's intelligence and sharp looks overpowered his intense religious practice, but deep down I had a gut feeling that Jaleh would lack the ability to change him and she would have to live life his way.

I told myself about how I was overthinking it. Reza seemed like a great young man and we approved of him more than we approved of the others. He had so many amazing qualities. The more we got to know him, the more his flaws seemed to fade in our eyes. Of course, Reza never lied about his beliefs. From the very beginning, he made it clear that he wanted his future wife in complete hijab, which Jaleh was opposed to. I never wore a hijab, nor did my daughters. Hassan insisted that Reza was only twenty-one, so he'd change in the future and we should look at all his positive points.

Hassan was hoping that since Reza had lived in America for a while, it would have relaxed his extremely religious mind. Hassan had millions of hopes and dreams about Reza. He was thinking of opening a construction office and allowing Reza to be the engineer. In his mind, we'd grow it and set a nice future for Arash and Ashkan as well. He was too absorbed in his dreams and talked to me about them every night. We were completely blinded by our imaginations. Jaleh was smart enough to know that Reza's beliefs alone were not grounds to make him the wrong husband for her. But we were almost certain that she was against the idea just to refuse to marry.

We said yes to Reza's family without Jaleh's approval, which was very selfish of us and unfair to Jaleh.

She was upset about the upcoming wedding. She did not show any signs of being impressed when we told her about Reza, and all the positive things we saw in him. She just kept repeating, "Do not do this to me; he is not the right choice. I do not want to marry!" over and over again. We grew tired of hearing it, but we learned to tune out her disapproval and thought of all the benefits of getting her married.

We did the same to Jaleh that my parents had done to me. They had just kicked me out and did not even listen or care. They called me a kid who did not know what was best for me. I see now that it was almost the same. Jaleh was the one who was going to spend the rest of her life with him and she had every right to argue and fight us, but we never listened. We just forced her to the point that she gave up fighting and just became quiet. But never for a second did she accept it, not for a second did she let her guard down and give in. Hassan and I wished she realized that we knew marriage was not something she wanted, but it was exactly what she needed.

But now I see that as parents, we should have cared more and supported her in what she really wanted. We should've taken responsibility and stood by our child and found the best path for her future. If she was so against marriage, we should've thought of another way. All I could think of at that time was to send her on the exact wrong path that Hassan and I were on. We did this to her. I did this to her.

We assured Jaleh that she would not lose anything, only her title would be a married woman. We told her that Reza was an educated young man and would not have any problems with her going back to school and continuing her education at the university. Hassan and I made sure to mention Jaleh's desire to continue her studies to Reza and he did not seem to have any problem with it.

The groom's family wanted the wedding ceremony very soon and they didn't see any reason to wait for months. They were in a rush and we thought that they were excited, which was something we did not mind either. We wanted the wedding to be held in Shiraz, where our families lived. We needed to find a location for the engagement ceremony, which is the responsibility of the bride's family. We needed to plan everything as soon as possible. Our house in Shiraz was not big enough for such a huge party.

For a second we had the idea to hold the engagement ceremony there, but the house was practically empty because we had stored everything away to prevent dust building up during the three seasons when we were gone. It would also be extra work to have to place all the pieces of furniture back in their original places, and get decorations on top of that. So we decided another location would be a smarter choice for the rushed ceremony.

My mother kept suggesting that we could have the engagement ceremony at her house, reminding Hassan and me about the beautiful garden, the pool, and lots of space at their home for our whole family to congregate. She was right; the garden at her home was a beautiful setting for a romantic occasion and the pool was fun too. On top of that there was more than enough space for the hundreds of family members that were expected to attend the engagement ceremony. I assumed that my mother was being kind and trying to help us out with the engagement, but I was wrong.

She acted as though a total stranger was holding an engagement party at her house. She made me pay for the most unnecessary expenses that had nothing to do with my daughter's getting married. For two months prior to the wedding I had to pay for her garden maintenance, pool maintenance, her utility bills, the maids, on top of the actual engagement party costs. What really did not make sense to me was the fact that I had to pay for her utility bills and kids' clothes; those costs had absolutely nothing to do with Jaleh's engagement party. It was just my mother's way of taking advantage of me just like she did with everyone all her life.

I never told Hassan that I had to pay my mother to hold our daughter's engagement party at her house. I never once vented about my family to him. I always protected my mother's reputation, even though I knew her well. People only knew her appearance and not her real personality. But because of that I was embarrassed to tell Hassan that my mother was charging me so much for nothing and taking advantage of the situation. But I needed to figure out a way to pay for them without Hassan's knowing.

I knew that the best way to get money from Hassan was to exaggerate the prices of the things he knew I had to buy. If I bought a dress for one hundred, I would say it was three hundred so that I could use the extra two hundred to pay my mother. Although it really bothered me that she was making me pay for everything, I learned to accept it and did not really think about it.

When everything was planned and ready, my mother told me to buy Jaleh a wedding gift and say that it was from her. I thought she would have the decency to at least get my daughter a wedding gift, but she did not. I couldn't let my daughter receive nothing from her own grandmother. It would not only look bad for my mother, but it would harm the reputation of our entire family. So, I had to do it.

When Reza's family informed us that the wedding had been planned and they were ready, we sent out the invitations to all our close and distant family members and headed back to Bushehr to get Jaleh, because it was school season, to bring her to Shiraz and have her attend her engagement party and wedding. To our surprise, her hate for getting married had not faded at all. The closer we got to the big day, the angrier and more defensive she got. We had made a foolish decision to put our daughter's life and our own on a crazier and more difficult path.

We very selfishly expected Jaleh to smile and agree with our decisions for her. She never gave up on disagreeing. As much as watching her suffer hurt us inside, Hassan and I kept ourselves firm and did not let her see what we felt.

Jaleh really kept making it harder and harder for us to marry her off. When we were ready to drive down to Shiraz, she refused to get in the car. Hassan literally had to drag her out of the house while she grabbed on to everything to keep herself from leaving. She grasped the drapes with both hands and held on so tight that with Hassan's dragging, it took down the curtains. He stuffed her into the car with difficulty, like she was a true prisoner who was innocent but was going to be executed anyway. We drove off to Shiraz, only days away from the ceremonies. How could I let that happen? I could have stood up and done something to prevent it all, but I never tried. I really thought it was the best thing for her at the time. The last thing that she said before she finally stopped fighting was, "I will never forgive you both."

We could have just tried harder to ban her from reading and watched over her and supervised her more. I was to be blamed. I was supposed to be there for her, but I was so busy enjoying my boys and my education that I forgot about my girls. I was not seeing that. I never saw that.

I was enjoying the prospect of her upcoming wedding and Hassan was very proud to have such a perfect son-in-law. We could easily see the differences between Reza and Jaleh, but had closed our eyes and dreamed and forced ourselves to see how everything was perfect or would be perfect someday soon. And once again, one more girl was to be sacrificed due to her parents' blindness.

We drove back to Shiraz without hearing a word from her. She was so quiet that the distance between Bushehr and Shiraz seemed like a century. She was so angry that her face seemed like it was about to explode. She tried so hard to stop us from making such a big mistake.

I was very scared; somewhere deep in my heart I knew something wasn't right.

Chapter 17

When Jaleh walked in, dressed in a white wedding gown, all the guests were stunned by her beauty. She looked like a gorgeous princess.

I stared at Jaleh, as she stood in the distance gazing at everyone who was attending her wedding. She looked zoned out and weak. I remembered my wedding, and how I had faked a smile for so long until my jaws could not bear it anymore. I remembered my thoughts and the uneasiness and I knew Jaleh was experiencing the same thing. I wondered if my smile was as bogus and unconvincing as hers. I wondered if people could see the unhappiness and frustration in my eyes when I smiled, like they could see in hers. I could sense that she was giving up on her strength; she was becoming weak with each passing second. Her chest kept expanding and contracting with sighs; I could tell she was simply giving up. I could tell she was hopeless. I could see the fear in her big, gorgeous eyes.

Reza looked very handsome that night. He was very quiet and barely smiled all night long. It was a glamorous and grand wedding, and an amazing night. But Reza did not appreciate parties because of his deeper religious beliefs. He wanted simplicity. He did not want Jaleh to be without a hijab and he was not very happy about it.

Although I knew Jaleh was unhappy, I was very happy and almost in tears that my daughter was getting married because after all it was a huge step up in life. She was all grown up. And that was it. I just felt like she wasn't seeing the bright side of it. Jaleh considered it a step down, but Hassan and I knew that soon her life would be transformed into something wonderful. We thought that everything would go better from that point in our lives. Jaleh would finally stop her political research and focus on her new life.

Jaleh moved into her new home. The house was built by Reza. It was his first project as an engineer; the property was gifted to them by Reza's father. It was a beautiful four-bedroom, one-story house.

I considered it romantic that the home he and his wife were going to spend the rest of their lives in, was the first building he had designed. The location of their home was rather unusual; it was placed on a piece of land where Reza's family lived. His parents and siblings all had separate homes on that land, but with no walls or divisions between them. They were all near one another, divided by gardens and little ponds, creeks and many different fruit trees. The whole area was private and bordered by walls. At the entrance to the land, there was an opening gate. The first home near the entrance of the property was Reza's parents'. They had the entire view of the entrance and observed everyone who entered and left the land.

For about two weeks everything in terms of Jaleh's marriage went well. She seemed fine living with Reza, and Hassan and I were glad everything was going normally and smoothly. As their marriage was arranged during the war between Iran and Iraq, all the men in Iran were conscripted. We had kept the war issue in mind, but we knew highly educated people had the option of helping Iran with the war in other ways rather than being on the battlefield. For instance, they could help heal the wounded if they had a background in medicine, or they could help plan attacks and organize groups, or as engineers they could build roads and bridges and many other things. That was why we knew that Reza did not have to be on the battlefield directly.

What we thought would not be a problem became one of the biggest problems in Jaleh and Reza's relationship. With no heads-up or prior mentioning, Reza left to fight for Iran within two weeks of his marriage to Jaleh. It was not because he had to; it was because he volunteered to. It was his wish and desire to fight at the frontline. Even though he had the option to not fight on the battlefield and risk his life, he chose to risk his life for martyrdom.

As we fit the puzzle pieces of Reza's unordinary actions together, we discovered a devastating truth. Reza was a part of a group that believed that if a man had a wife, and died in war, he would go straight to heaven. He only married Jaleh because he needed a wife for his religious theory to work.

We were deceived. All the urgency Reza's family had for the marriage ceremony to happen as soon as possible was for Reza to reach his goal of martyrdom sooner. He told us that he was religious, but he never explained his intentions. We were trying to protect Jaleh from getting involved in any such groups, and instead we tied her with one. We handed her to a man who was a part of one.

What had we done? She told us that she would never forgive us. She had many reasons not to. In trying to solve a small problem we only created a bigger one. We pushed our daughter into a whirlpool of disaster. We did that to her. She should never forgive us.

When Reza departed for the frontline he left some strict and unfair restrictions behind.

As if the thought of that was not hard enough on Jaleh, Reza had also banned her from going to school and visiting her family when he was gone. He told Jaleh that she absolutely had no right to leave the house while he was gone. She was to stay at home while he put his life at risk.

He wanted to go to heaven while he had a prisoner who he made sure to torture during his absence.

Everything that had happened to me was repeating itself in a different way.

Why? I had suffered enough. Why was my daughter supposed to go down the same sad road?

When he left, Jaleh's strength kicked in again. She was going to go back to school while Reza was gone and pray and hope for his return. She left the house even though he had told her not to. Reza's parents' perfect view of the entrance of their little neighborhood gate interfered with Jaleh s plan to leave without being noticed.

We also found out that Reza's parents were well aware of his intentions of going to war. They knew that the only reason he wanted a wife was to complete the equation of what he believed would take him to heaven. They knew he went to war to be a martyr. They knew everything, and they let him marry an innocent fifteen-year-old girl who was soon to be a widow because of their son's selfish, pathetic, and disgusting theory. That was why they were completely on Reza's side and they did not want Jaleh to leave the house for any reason because they considered it betrayal.

Reza used to call his parents from the war zone once in a while, but he never called his wife. Jaleh waited for a few months and could not find any reason to stay. She did not let Reza's family stop her from leaving. We picked her up and she came and lived with us back in Bushehr while Reza was gone.

Despite the fact that they were only together for two weeks, Jaleh had grown strong and powerful feelings for him. So you would think that a girl who fought with all her might to not get married would not be so troubled by the thought of her husband leaving for war, but those assumptions were wrong. The girl who did all that fighting fell in love, and had her heart broken.

We felt ashamed that she went through all that because of us, but we knew that if Reza had honestly explained his reason for desiring for this marriage we would have never let it happen. Reza was young, and we felt like he didn't know what he was doing; he was just making a grave mistake. But we could never forgive or even come to understand his parents' hypocrisy and betrayal. How could they let their son get married with that goal in mind? Jaleh came home weak and tired emotionally. She loved Reza and all she wanted was for him to come back home again, healthy and safe.

But that was not his plan. For all we knew, he might never come back. Jaleh hated how he did not let her go to school or see her family and made her stay at home as a pre-widow. She could not understand why he limited her to just staying at home and waiting for him. She did not follow by his rules, and she did not even understand why they were there in the first place.

Hassan was devastated. We all were so worried. There could be a bad phone call with that unpleasant news any moment. Hassan was regretting the way he ruined Jaleh's life in the blink of an eye.

We started to blame him for everything, disregarding the fact that I myself was a part of that mistake. Our life turned completely upside down. We had Jaleh back with a load of pressure on her that we were responsible for. Hassan worried that his fifteen-year-old daughter was going to become a widow, and he would be the reason for it. We were to be blamed for ruining her youth. Jaleh was right and I knew it. She would, and should, never forgive us.

Jaleh and I regularly called Reza's mother to see if he had come home. We were clueless about when he would return. Reza never cared to contact Jaleh, so we kept calling Reza's parents because they obviously would be the first ones to find out, and we wanted them to give us a heads-up.

A few months had passed and every time we called, their answers remained the same, that he called, and he was fine. But too much time had passed, and we knew that the soldiers had breaks to come back home for a visit. Reza could not have been the only one without that privilege.

We figured that could not be possible. How could there be no news at all?!

Once when we had called Reza's parents, they were not at home, and Sherry had picked up the phone.

Reza's brother had a very kind wife named Sherry. They had been married for almost ten years and she knew her mother-in-law was heartless. So we decided to ask Sherry, who was also Jaleh's neighbor, if Reza had returned. Sherry was very nice, and acted like Jaleh's older sister. She was six years older than Jaleh and always wanted to help Jaleh out, and because she was honest, she told Jaleh that Reza had already returned home twice in these few months, and he always called ahead to inform his parents, but they did not tell Jaleh.

"We did not know they had kept it a secret from you and until tonight we assumed you did not want him anymore," she said and added she would have called Jaleh if she knew what was going on. She felt extremely sorry for her and said that Reza was still there and told us to try to get to Shiraz as soon as possible.

His parents had lied to us, saying that he had not come back because they wanted to punish Jaleh for leaving without Reza's permission.

How could they think of a punishment in this situation? A young wife, worried about her husband who was at the frontline in a dangerous war was not punishment enough for her?

Hassan and I drove Jaleh to Shiraz right after that conversation. We went to Reza's parents' home and confronted them and asked them why they would not tell their son's wife that her husband had come home from war.

They told us to our faces that she did not deserve to see him. When we asked why, they said that she did not do as Reza had told her. He had asked her to stay at home and wait for him to return without visiting her family, and the first thing she did was to go back to us and leave the home that Reza had provided for her.

How could they expect a fifteen-year-old girl to sit at home alone and lonely, and wait for her husband to return?

Couldn't they at least give her the permission to go home to her family while he was gone? I could not even understand their logic. I did not see the reasoning behind it. They were very cold and heartless when they spoke to us. They were certain that they were right. They couldn't care less about how Jaleh felt. Jaleh was nobody to them, just a wife who was a ticket for their son's entrance to heaven. When Reza found out that Jaleh had left home even though he had banned her from doing so, he did not want to see her. He would only see her if he knew she followed his orders. But after a good confrontation, they allowed Jaleh to return home to her husband for the remaining weeks that he had left staying home, before he had to leave to war again.

I couldn't handle what was happening. Neither could Hassan. I told Hassan that Reza was his punishment from God. I told him that he was suffering because of the years of oppression, cruelty, selfishness, and unfairness that he treated me with. "Reza is just like you," I told him. "Why should my daughter pay for your sins and crimes?" I cried.

After Jaleh was allowed to go back to her husband, everything seemed fine. Everything had mellowed down to a neutral mode. With Reza at home, Jaleh spent a lot of time together with him, and shortly before his next departure to war Jaleh announced that she was pregnant. The news destroyed Hassan. "We will get Jaleh a divorce from him and will send her out of the country for education," He had told me before he found out about her pregnancy, and also told her many times.

Jaleh refused and kept saying, "Now that I love him? You forced me to marry him, I had told you from the beginning that he is not my match, but you were blind to see the truth. It is too late now, and divorce is not the solution."

Jaleh seemed hopeful and determined, thinking that with a child on the way, Reza would change his dream of dying in war and think about his wife and the child's future and would stay in Shiraz. It reminded me of the time when I had announced I was pregnant for the first time, and how much impact it had on Hassan, how much of a better husband he slowly became from that day forward. We expected that Reza would call off his next departure to war because Jaleh was pregnant and he needed to be there for her.

That thought that we did not have to worry about him losing his life on the battlefield brought relief to almost everyone. But that was when our and Jaleh's hopes turned into the same gloomy reality we were all used to living.

Reza announced that he was still going to war, but that Jaleh would be allowed to go to our house during her pregnancy, but had to be back whenever he came home if he ever came back at all. His declaration shocked us. We were almost certain that he would not leave his pregnant wife to go to war. We were again reminded of his intentions of going to war. We knew that he was hoping to die with the expectation of going to heaven.

Reza's mother and father did not even try to stop him. They did not even once say, "You should not leave behind your pregnant wife and instead should stay and work in Shiraz." Hassan and I knew that they felt no pity toward our daughter. It was as if they were proud of their son. That was when hate grew in Jaleh's heart for Reza's mother and father. We were never impolite to them, and neither was Jaleh. If Reza's mother were a nice human being, things would have been different. At least it would not have been as bad as it was because he would have listened to his mother. She would have been able to change the situation to make it at least a little better, but she had no compassion or mercy. When Reza left for war, Jaleh moved in with us. We were her better choice, but she was not very fond of us either.

"Are you happy now? Did you get what you wanted? Are you relieved that I am married?" she screamed daily. She reminded Hassan and me every single day about how we ruined her life, and how we destroyed her and how we could never look into her eyes for the rest of our lives. She screamed at us, got angry, and cried every single day.

I wish she knew that we never intended for her life to turn out this way; we never meant for her to have a hard marriage. "My husband is gone, I am carrying a baby, and any minute I may get a message stating that he is dead!" Her anger was more of a sadness, depression, and fear. I could see that all those feelings built up inside of her, which made her want to scream the way she did every day. She feared that Reza would die.

"Divorce him, Jaleh. Get yourself out of this awful marriage!" Hassan told her.

"Now you want me to get a divorce, while there is a baby on the way? You want me to live the rest of my life far away from my child; they will take him or her from me. The law won't let me keep my child. It is too late. I would be a widowed mother. Is that the life you wanted me to live?" Her words silenced us. We knew that it was too late for anything; everything had turned into a catastrophe. We had fallen into a pothole that there was no getting out of it. It was like Jaleh was tied up to a dartboard and everybody was throwing darts at her. She could not take it. I could see it in her eyes that she was fed up. She was really beginning to hate life. She was disgusted by everything that had to do with her existence. She hated Reza's parents and never visited them when he was not home. She was losing herself in her thoughts, and the hole we dug for her and pushed her in purposely. Our life was just like a broken ship in an unexpected storm and each one of us was holding only a piece to stay on top and be able to breathe; we were not living, we were just alive.

Chapter 18

JALEH SPENT HER ENTIRE PREGNANCY IN STRESS, DEPRESSION, and anxiety, and we spent it in shame and sorrow.

She stopped blaming us and screaming at us. She stopped crying and that was what made us even sorrier.

We could have gone with our plan A, which had always been Hassan's wish to send our daughters to another country to study. Why didn't we just do that? Why did we destroy her life and ours?

Hassan took Jaleh, Arash, Ashkan, and me to our Shiraz home for a few months before her labor to be close to the doctors. Since it was school time, he went back to Bushehr with Laleh. A lot of time had passed that I was away from Laleh. We had no time or headspace to care for her. That was how I scattered my family; at that moment there was nothing else we could do.

When Jaleh was nine months pregnant, Reza's mother informed him that the baby was on its way, and Reza returned home for the delivery. The only person Reza communicated with while he was at war was his mother. Even when he had the chance, he did not care to call Jaleh and see how she was doing. We were surprised that he would even plan to be there for when Jaleh was giving birth. But no man could ever be that shallow. Not even Reza as it turned out.

Jaleh went into a very hard labor. The pain she felt for many hours was excruciating and challenging to take. She suffered as she felt contractions over and over again. It reminded me of the pain I went through when I was pregnant with her. She was my first child and I was fourteen when I had her, and she was sixteen when having her first child. As she was carrying a very heavy, ten-pound baby, it made giving birth for her very difficult. After more than fourteen hours of labor, the doctors realized that she needed a cesarean. After a long wait in the waiting room while she was in the operating room, the doctor came out and said the baby had been successfully delivered and that we could see it. It was a beautiful big baby boy with long black hair, who looked like Reza. He was very adorable and loving, my first grandson.

In that moment, it hit me that I was officially a grandmother. I was a grandmother at the age of thirty, which is kind of odd, but I was more than joyous. Reza had decided to name him Ali, a beautiful name for a beautiful boy.

It was not a surprise that shortly after Ali was born, Reza left for war again. Not even Ali's life could change his mind to stop thinking only about his desires. "You are a father now. Your responsibility is completely different," we told him, but he left regardless.

Jaleh came to our home with Ali. Arash was an uncle at the age of six and Ashkan a cute uncle at the age of one and a half. Laleh was fourteen when she was left behind for years and the only thing she was expected to do was take care of her brothers and that was not something she really wanted to do. Because of that, she was mostly angry and complained a lot. But there was no other choice; our life was in such a mess and I needed her help. She had turned into a babysitter for our family and it was not fair to her. We were all working hard to deal with the disaster that we had created.

Every time Reza visited, we all knew that he would leave again because the only reason he went back was to die. That was why Jaleh would get more and more depressed every time that he left because she felt like he just did not care about her or their son. And there was no way to change his mind. She had thought that maybe the feeling of being a father to Ali would be the reason that would keep Reza home, but she was wrong. The only thing that he cared about was dying and going to heaven.

I was sure that if he died in the war, he would not go to heaven, not after what he had done to Jaleh. We as people may be blinded by our made-up lies, but God is not. We all pay the price for our mistakes.

The end of Jaleh's story was too obvious. Jaleh would eventually have to raise Ali alone, with nothing to hope for. Her life got to a point where at such a young age, she felt as though there was nothing to live for, nothing to be happy about. For her, there was no light at the end of the tunnel to run toward. She had nowhere to go; she just decided to stay in one spot.

Even with Ali, she packed up and moved in with us every time Reza left. She did not want to live alone in a home that was near Reza's inquisitive and disrespectful mother. Jaleh did not go to visit them and they never visited her either, even to see Ali.

On a summer day after Reza's last visit, Jaleh came back home seeming very different. She was disappointed and sad. As days passed by, we noticed that Jaleh was becoming duller and extremely quiet. After a few days she started acting weird about everything and it seemed that the only thing she wanted was to go back and live alone with Ali. She insisted that she wanted to be in her own home and did not need us to go with her.

It was bizarre because she always refused to live there while Reza was gone, but this time she was practically begging for us to let her go back. "I want to go back home with Ali and stay there forever. That is my destiny and that's where I should be. I belong there." We couldn't understand why she wanted to go back. We didn't know what made her change so suddenly. But there was no reason to stop her. It was her home after all, so we let her do as she wished, and we took her back. Since it was summer we stayed in our Shiraz home. We were closer to her and thought we could see her every day, so maybe it wasn't a bad idea for her to settle in her home and start getting used to living there.

When she got home, shortly after we left, she told Reza's mother to look after Ali because she was tired, and she wanted to go and rest. Without giving Reza's mother any time to react, she left Ali with her and went back to her house. Reza's mother was very shocked that Jaleh let her look after Ali because she knew how much Jaleh disliked her.

For around an hour, she was thinking about why Jaleh would ever let her have him without Jaleh around. Her suspicions and curiosity were driving her mad, and she had a feeling that something was wrong. She told Sherry to go and see if Jaleh was okay because she had a weird feeling that Jaleh was acting strange. When Sherry went to Jaleh's home, she found her on her bed, unconscious. Beside her lay an empty bottle of sleeping pills that she had stolen from Reza's mother. Her body was limp. Her paleness was frightening. My own daughter had attempted suicide. Sherry noticed that Jaleh was still breathing and holding on to life. She instantly called an ambulance and Jaleh was rushed to the hospital. When Hassan and I received the phone call from Sherry from the hospital, our world came completely crashing down. I did not know whether to scream, cry, or just smash everything that was surrounding me. Fear rushed inside of me. So much had gone wrong in my own baby girl's life. I felt a pain I had never felt before. No matter what I had gone through in the past, nothing came close to hearing about my own daughter's choosing to die rather than live another day in this world. I wanted so much for her, but never this. I had to control my emotions. I didn't want to scream or cry. We had to be careful with our actions because we didn't want the kids to find out what had happened to their sister. Like always, we had to leave Arash and Ashkan with Laleh. She was so frustrated, but we had no other choice.

We drove down to the hospital with the fear of hearing the news that Jaleh had died. Hassan couldn't have driven any faster. We both knew that every second counted. During the drive, a million things were running through my head.

We went through all this to prevent her from joining any of the political groups so that we could keep her alive. And now we had driven her to the point where life was completely painful and worthless for her. There was no point of it anymore. We killed her soul two years ago and now we took her life.

When we got there, Sherry was the only one with her; none of Reza's family members were at the hospital. They tortured my daughter and left her all alone. Sherry said with teary eyes that doctors were trying very hard to save her.

We sat in the hospital, waiting. We tried figuring out a way to lie to Laleh because we did not want her to know what her older sister had done. We didn't want it to influence her in any way. She would only learn that if anything went wrong she could just take her life and choose the easiest way out and never fight back.

Along with keeping the tragedy from Laleh, Hassan and I decided to keep it from our entire family as well because it would bring great sorrow and shame to our family.

We always maintained our family's reputation, and as hard as it was, we knew that for the sake of our family's image, we had to do all that we could to keep it a secret.

The chemicals in the pills had caused severe damage to the walls of her stomach, which led to continuous internal bleeding and major acid reflux. The news was devastating and disturbing, making us imagine how much of a painful way it was to die. However, we knew that it was a pain she could not feel because she was in a coma, half-dead.

What really bothered us and crushed our hearts was the fact that Reza had put Jaleh through such a tragedy and his family did not even care to be beside her. She was in a coma and we did not even know if she would ever wake up. That night I witnessed the biggest miracle in my life to this day.

The doctors came out and told us that Jaleh was going to be okay. I cried very hard as soon as I heard the news. I thought the doctors would come back with bad news. I felt like God was giving our family a second chance to make things right. I knew in my heart that I was never going to let my baby get to that point in life again. The doctors told us that Jaleh was mentally and emotionally a wreck and that when she woke up from the coma and recovered fully, we would have to give her our full attention and treat her with the most respect that we could so that she would feel like she belonged somewhere and everyone appreciated her existence. The problem was that she needed comfort, attention, and love from Reza and he could not care less about her feelings.

As soon as Jaleh fully recovered from her coma, she came back home as a new person. I reminded Hassan to treat her with as much respect and alertness to her emotions as he could because she was emotionally damaged. The first thing that Hassan did when he saw Jaleh was beat her and verbally demolish all the strength she had left in her soul. I could tell that he broke her. I tried to stop him, but I couldn't. He easily pushed me away every time. I was powerless when he was like this. It was his way of showing his fear of losing her, and his frustration with how his daughter was so depressed and emotionally destroyed. He beat her with all his strength. His demons had come back because of all the pressure that he'd felt. He left Jaleh wishing she were dead. All I could do was stay by her side and cry as he hurt her, just as Jaleh had sat by my side when she was little, and cried when Hassan had hit me.

A day or two after Jaleh came home and none of Reza's family cared to visit or even call, Reza's brother unexpectedly came to our home with a message from Reza's family. They wanted a divorce and would not give Ali back to her because they were ashamed that Jaleh had tried to commit suicide.

As soon as he said that, I completely lost my temper. I let all my anger out. I screamed louder than I had ever screamed. I spoke words I never thought I would speak. I yelled so much that I could hardly breathe. "You people are the reason my daughter tried to commit suicide! You people are the reason she is an emotional mess! Your mistreatments broke her heart until there was nothing left but the shattered pieces! You took her soul and trapped it in a cage! You made her life miserable! You lied to us! You never once mentioned martyrdom! He did not need a victim to be dragged down with him! He could have just gone to war and pursued his dreams! He could've died alone! You dragged us into your misery! And now after all that, you do not want her anymore?! You should be ashamed of yourselves that you caused her to attempt and even *think* about taking her own life! All the shame is on you for treating a sixteen-year-old this carelessly. How heartless could a family be to send such a message instead of caring for a young girl's life? You people are pathetic. I would be embarrassed to even show my face if I were you. I would be the most embarrassed human being alive knowing I destroyed a family all because of my obnoxious mistreatments and stupid beliefs! You got some nerve coming here at all!" Even Hassan was surprised at the words that were coming out of my mouth. The whole room went silent and all of a sudden Reza's brother became polite. I could see that shame was changing the color of his skin. He was humiliated.

He went home and brought Ali back to Jaleh. He found Reza and asked him to come home and he did. Jaleh was getting better. She felt extremely sorry for what she had done, and she was happy to be alive for Ali's sake. She realized that Ali was all she needed and wanted.

Unfortunately, even Jaleh's failed suicide attempt did not send a message to Reza, and he did not stop going to war for his death. Not too long after she had started to heal, he left for war once again.

Any love and care that Jaleh had left for Reza was lost. Her only hope was Ali. She went from a girl who fought for what she wanted, to a girl who did not care because she knew she could not change anything no matter how hard she tried. Her life was over. Everything kept going downhill, until it dropped into the deep end where we all were drowning.

Hassan asked her yet again to divorce Reza, promising to send her abroad to study that and everyone would forget about what had happened to us as if it were just a nightmare.

Jaleh said she did not love Reza, not even a little, but if she got divorced his family would take Ali away from her. In Iranian law, fathers get custody of the child after divorce. She did not want a minute of her life without Ali in it. "I will suffer beside a maniac just to be with Ali," she said.

Chapter 19

JALEH'S FUTURE AND HAPPINESS WERE GONE BECAUSE OF our mistakes and foolishness and now she chose to sacrifice the rest of her youth waiting for Reza to come home as a dead body. She started wishing for Reza to reach his martyrdom sooner. She had Ali and that was all that mattered to her. But to Hassan, waiting for that day was killing him from within. He was so sorry that he could not change Reza, as he had said he would before their marriage. He was sorry that he ruined Jaleh's life and destroyed ours in the process too. Maybe he saw himself in Reza, the man he was when we got married. He could not believe that Jaleh would not really care if Reza came home dead. He knew she cared and she was dying inside and suffering and was just smiling for Ali's sake. Hassan was broken so bad that nothing could gather the scattered pieces of his soul. I had never seen him so sad.

I asked Hassan to change our drapes, as the pattern and style of them were bothering me and getting on my nerves. He always refused doing any chore that had to do with heights. He feared heights more than anybody I knew. "You do it; you know I am afraid of stepping on a stool. What if it tips over and I fall?" Although his words frustrated me, I accepted changing the drapes myself. The littlest things were bothering everyone. It was not just the drapes or the sound of a clock ticking; it was simply everything. Nothing felt right anymore. Everything felt out of place and was improper. Everything in our surroundings was just incorrect.

We did not have any souls in our bodies. We all were just living corpses.

We gave up on persuading Reza to stay home; he proved to us that his beliefs were unchangeable. Reza reminded us of a drug addict you could not force to stop unless he truly wanted to. Reza did not want to stop going to war. He did not want to stop at all, and so he proved we were powerless and our efforts were useless.

Jaleh's shadow seemed to follow us everywhere. There was this darkness in her shadow that blocked us from the light of happiness. The shadow that followed us was the sorrow we had caused her. Every breath that we took was a sigh, not of relief but of depression. When Jaleh looked at us, we looked down in disgrace.

When she looked at us in her silence, we could feel her scream and cry from within. The life she lived put a permanent tear in her eyes that blurred her vision from seeing any happiness at all. And when we looked her in the eyes, we could see the sadness that she felt.

The most depressed person among us all seemed to be Hassan. Not that he sat in a corner and didn't speak. He just gave up on a lot of things we never thought he would give up on. He would pray regularly, in honor of practicing the Muslim religion, but ever since he realized that Reza was causing so much pain to Jaleh using religion as an excuse, the thought of religion sickened him.

Hassan had not missed a day of prayer all his life, but after the tragedy of Jaleh's suicide attempt, he put all his religious beliefs aside. I knew that he was broken and hurt because he forced Jaleh to get married and hit her when she desperately needed love and attention. I felt like he regretted it, and the feeling of guilt was eating him up inside. He knew that we did this to her.

The emptiness in our broken family turned into a routine. It formed its own normality and lifestyle, a lifestyle we were all following without a choice. Although Jaleh was beside me, I got the vibe that her soul was not there. That was when I knew I had to use all the stored happiness that I had left inside of me, to make Jaleh's life a little better. I knew that her lack of energy, emotionally and physically, prevented her from taking care of Ali properly. That was the only thing I could think of to help Jaleh through her pain. Everything I tried for Jaleh seemed like taking only a little weight off the tons that she carried on her shoulders. But I did the best that I could to take away her worries related to Ali. I did everything for Ali and I loved him very much.

After a month of being on the battlefield, which seemed like decades, Reza returned home again. Because I had exploded with anger on Reza's family before with no hesitation, they regularly updated us when Reza was going to return. Jaleh would follow her routine of moving back in with him for the time that he stayed, before his next departure to war. He usually came home after three months and stayed for a week or two. But in the summers, he came twice. When Jaleh left our home, we continued living life in the same low-spirited way that we did when she was there. Hassan refused to see Reza and did not want him at our house at all. He informed me that he could not stand to be in the presence of his chosen son-in-law.

I woke up one morning exhausted, feeling like I had slept on a strainer the whole night and all of my energy and might had sunk into the bed. As I walked around half-alive and present, Hassan suggested that I should go to the doctor. "Laleh, take your mother along with Arash and Ashkan to see a doctor. Your mom seems weak and in need of a checkup," Hassan insisted.

"I am fine, Hassan. I am just tired, nothing serious enough to go to the doctor's for," I argued. I was not really sick, and I knew it was all because of the mental pressures we had been through, and I did not understand why he wanted me to go to the doctor so much. Every time I said no he brought it up again and said I had to go. Maybe he really wanted to show that he cared after all we had been through.

"I have some things to fix up in the house anyways; I would have something to do while you guys are gone," Hassan said. He insisted that I should take the kids with me so that they could tag along and have something to do. I kept asking myself why he wanted me to leave so badly to go see a doctor I did not even need. It seemed like he was dealing with his emotions this way. We had all changed after everything that had happened with Jaleh, and it seemed like Hassan was changing for the better that day. He just really wanted to see me healthy and well.

"Laleh, your mother is being stubborn. Take her to the doctor's. She just does not want to admit that she needs it," he insisted. He told Laleh, who was only fourteen, to be in charge. I finally decided to go to please Hassan. I took the kids to the door and stood at the doorway. We all looked at Hassan to say our goodbyes. He stared at the kids in the most loving way, more loving than he had ever looked at anything in his life. I stared at his expression as he kneeled to the floor where our two-year-old Ashkan stood. He grabbed him by the waist and lifted him up to the air and stared at him as he held him up high to the ceiling. "You are so adorable. I love you so much and I will miss you." He spoke the words his tongue never felt comfortable with before. He then squeezed Arash into his chest and hugged him as a tear built up in his eye and said, "Take care of your mother." I looked at him and I knew he was a different man. The man I saw was not Hassan. He never showed his love the way he was showing it toward us in the doorway. His goodbye was unusual for a few hours' trip to the doctor's. His goodbye was too heartfelt to be ignored. He truly loved his kids, but he never told them directly that he loved them. I was scared.

"We are not going anywhere," I stated. "If you want me to go to the doctor's so bad, come with us." I stood with my hands crossed on my chest. I looked strong, but I felt worried, confused, and weak. My mind could not process what was going on.

"Don't be silly, darling, just go to the doctor!" he insisted, sounding a little demanding.

"Yeah, Mom, quit being so stubborn and let's go already!" Laleh encouraged. Hassan walked us to the car and followed us to the end of the alley, and when I looked back he had vanished.

"He is gone, where did he go?" I said panicking.

"Calm down. He told us he was going to do chores in the house. Will you relax?" Laleh disputed. I kept looking back and forth; I kept looking back until my view of the house had faded. And then I continued on my way to the doctor's.

We got to the clinic and the waiting room was full. We sat there for a long time until the doctor finally saw me and told me I was fine, obviously. I was ready to go home and tell Hassan, "See, I told you I did not need to visit the doctor!"

The sky had turned dark and the moon had lit up the streets. The stars were starting to become visible when we got home. We stood behind the glass entrance doors; the glass was a blurry window in which you could vividly see the inside of our home.

"See, Father's right there. How many times did I tell you that you were worrying for no reason?" Laleh ranted as she gazed into the window as I unlocked the door. When we walked in, there we saw Hassan. Laleh was right; he was there after all, with his neck in a red rope noose, hanging from the high ceiling of our home.

His head, fingers, and toes all pointed to the ground, and his pajamas draped over his lifeless body. A shock filled up our bodies that weakened our knees and made us want to drop to the floor. A rage that was full of defeat ran through my blood and made me scream. Tears poured down our eyes uncontrollably as I ran up to him and hugged him as we released his neck from the rope. I did not know what to do; I dropped to the ground grasping his head on my lap, rocking him back and forth while crying. He had been dead for a long time. Laleh, Arash, and Ashkan saw an image no child should ever see. Their father had hung himself. I did not think it was possible to cry and scream as loud as all four of us did. So loud that it worried the neighbors and made them run into our home to see what was going on. We dealt with every wound life had cut into us; we were too weak to deal with a cut so deep. This time, life's knife stabbed us straight through the heart and pulled it out.

We sat in our home with what was left of Hassan in our laps, surrounded by a crowd that stared down at us. I wondered what they saw; I wondered what their eyes limited them to see. I wondered if just by looking at us, they saw what we had really experienced. I wondered if they knew how much worse the scene was than it seemed. I wondered if they could tell how Hassan could not face Jaleh anymore, that he wasn't able to look her in the eyes if they brought Reza's body to her.

What about me, Hassan?!

What about Laleh?!

What about Arash and Ashkan?!

God, what a journey...

What would be next?!

CPSIA information can be obtained
at www.ICGtesting.com
Printed in the USA
LVHW091338120320
649854LV00001B/99

9 789176 375532